The Three Sisters

Tum-Bak-Tee

Wapsno
River

Pal-Chin Mountains

Land of
Sarop the Great

Sarop's Castle

Ogewo

Learning from HANNAH

Learning from HANNAH

~ Secrets for a
Life Worth Living

William H. Thomas, M.D.

VanderWyk & Burnham
Acton, Massachusetts

Published by VanderWyk & Burnham
A Division of Publicom, Inc.
P.O. Box 2789, Acton, Massachusetts 01720

This book is available for quantity purchases. For information on bulk discounts, call (800) 789-7916 or write to Special Sales at the above address.

Library of Congress Cataloging-in-Publication Data
Thomas, William H., M.D.
    Learning from Hannah : secrets for a life worth living / William H. Thomas, M.D.
        p.   cm.
    ISBN 1-889242-09-8
    I. Title.
PS3570.H59225L43   1999
813'.54—dc21   98-54732
                                                              CIP

Interior illustrations by Lenice U. Strohmeier
Map illustration by Roberto Osti
Book design by Ruth Lacey Design

Manufactured in the United States of America
10 9 8 7 6 5 4 3 2 1

Dedicated to all of my children,
born and yet to be born

All work is a seed sown;
it grows and spreads,
and sows itself anew.

—Carlyle

Contents

Prologue

W<small>HEN</small> I <small>WAS A BOY</small>, my eyes were open to the magic in this world. I knew that if I jumped high enough, I could touch the sun, the moon, and the stars. They belonged to me and I loved them. Unfortunately, my tendency to daydream exasperated my teachers. I was a poor student and their complaints were frequent. "He doesn't pay attention!" "He never finishes his homework!" "He wastes time!" "Why isn't he living up to his potential?"

I'd like to say I defied their calls for conformity and denied them their victory, but I did not. A child's imagination is no match for adults armed with good intentions. They taught me that my sun was a blast furnace, my moon a cold, dead rock, and my stars far beyond my reach. They cleansed me of my misconceptions, and the magic disappeared.

Ultimately, I embraced their faith in the majesty of science, and as converts often do, I became a fanatic. I earned a bachelor of science degree in biology, *summa cum laude,* and then a medical degree from Harvard. As a young physician, I believed that science would conquer all. Every corner of the human body, every crevice of the Earth, even the farthest reaches of the cosmos would yield their secrets to the scientific method, I was sure. It was only a matter of time.

All that confidence is gone now. It has been shattered and washed away.

My wife Jude and I had anticipated productive but commonplace lives when we married. Instead, we were torn from our world and transported by forces beyond our understanding to and from a place where magic lives in the hearts of everyone. Our old life, the people we were, the person I was taught to be—all of that is gone.

No scientist will ever be able to explain where we were. No rational explanation can be made to fit the facts. We entered, lived in for a year, and learned to love a land called Kallimos. We trod its paths, worked its soil, breathed its air, and drank its water. The desire to return to Kallimos has burned in our hearts since the night we left its shores. We want what we cannot have.

I do not know how or why we were chosen to travel there. I do know that Kallimos made Jude and me into new people. It was there that we received gentle instruction in the art of repairing our souls. We opened our hearts and our minds and, in doing so, we found new lives to live. We have set aside our former strivings and have taken up new work that is more meaningful and rewarding than anything we could have imagined. We have learned how to build a better world for our elders and ourselves.

We can teach you. We shall teach you, but first you must listen to our story. For me, the hardest part is finding the courage to tell this story. I am afraid you'll think that I'm crazy or at least deluded, that you'll dismiss my journal as a fraud, the product of an overheated imagination. Ten years ago, I would have done the same. After all, who has time for magical tales of adventure when real life is pressing in from all sides? Jude and I used to believe that the truth was the truth only when it was clothed in numbers and facts. We were wrong. The people of Kallimos taught us that the truth—that wisdom—comes to us dressed in stories. When we dismiss the stories, we deny ourselves the wisdom they contain, and our lives are the poorer for our foolishness.

Deciding to tell a story and knowing how to tell it are two different things. The people of Kallimos make it seem so easy. I find it very hard. I've lost count of the number of times I've rewritten this tale. In early drafts, I thought it would be best if I told you about our old lives. I described the small towns where we grew up, and I introduced our parents and siblings. I even described our first loves and heartbreaks. But all of the common-

3

place, perfectly normal events that made up our old lives did nothing to prepare us for what was to come. They do not explain what *we* have become. Perhaps the only way for you to understand how Kallimos has changed us is to read my journal. But before that, I will tell you how Jude and I met and what led us to sail toward Montserrat.

Rochester, New York

I SUPPOSE YOU COULD SAY everything really began when I met Jude. After medical school, I chose geriatrics as my specialty and began my residency at the University of Rochester. At the time, I dreamed of becoming a professor of medicine, and I hoped to make a name for myself as an author of medical textbooks. My ambitions led me to spend most of my off-call evenings in the medical library, poring over the most recently published research I could find. It was there that I met Jude.

Jude has a warm and gentle beauty that makes people want to get close to her. I will never forget the first time I saw her. She looked up from the book she was reading, and her bright brown eyes met my gaze. She smiled at me and I felt woozy. Her dress was dark green. Her long, chestnut brown hair fell down around her shoulders, and a silver necklace glittered against the green of her dress. I went outside to calm down and think of something I could say to her without sounding stupid. When I returned, she was gone. I cursed my luck.

I shouldn't have worried, because we were meant to be together. On my next visit to the library, she was there. It was crowded that night, and I asked if I could take a seat at her table. She said yes.

I learned that she was a gerontologist and that she was close to finishing her doctoral thesis on the interactions between social institutions and the elderly. Soon we were working at the same table every night, always side by side.

It didn't take us long to realize that our mutual interests encompassed more than the study of aging and the elderly, that we shared a passion for sailing. Thus, evenings in the library led to weekends on Lake Ontario. A faculty member who was going on sabbatical asked if we would boat-sit his 25-foot ketch. He didn't have to ask twice. We sailed her hard and well that year and won a basketful of trophies. We were married in September 1986.

After Jude finished her thesis and I finished my residency, the William's Gerontology Center offered us research fellowships. Specifically, the center asked us to write a textbook that integrated research on the medical aspects and the social aspects of aging. Certain that professional success lay straight ahead, we accepted, packed our bags, and moved to New York City. We poured ourselves into our work.

New York City

SNOW WAS FALLING SOFTLY on the street outside our apartment building when we completed our manuscript. It was a Monday morning after a sleepless Sunday night. We had worked around the clock in a frenzied final round of manuscript proofreading. The deadline had pushed us close to our breaking points. The clock read 6:29 A.M. when we finished The Book. That's what we called it—The Book. Officially, its title was *Medical and Social Aspects of Aging,* but to us it was The Book. We had worked on it side by side, six days a week, for two years. In our minds, it was nothing less than a 1,215-page tyrant, and it had ruled our lives.

The gray morning light of the city filtered in through the kitchen window to reveal the completed manuscript in its cardboard box on the kitchen table. It contained more than 500 graphs and over 700 tables. Footnotes? Don't even ask. We never did manage to count them all. The Book was our distillation of tens of thousands of research articles, monographs, and literature reviews. It contained, as of February 3, 1989, the sum of human knowledge about aging. I don't think we'll ever forget that date. Our publisher had drilled it into our heads as the "final and forever, do or die, drop-dead deadline." Now it was here, and we were ready to deliver what we had promised.

I slammed the lid down over the box and wrapped it with packing tape. When the last piece of tape was in place, we toasted our victory with the dregs from a carton of warm orange juice. The tyrant was caged, and we had just over three hours to spare. All I had to do was carry the boxed manuscript to our publisher's offices on West 57th Street.

The people in the apartment upstairs went through their morning ritual of floor-thumping and door-banging. Cars hissed like snakes as they slithered through the dirty slush. We just sat at our table. Neither of us moved or spoke for what seemed like a long time.

"It's over," I said.

Jude nodded her head slowly in agreement. We had often fantasized about throwing a wild party when we

9

had The Book behind us. Now that the day was here, we didn't have the energy to celebrate. Jude got up and walked over to the window.

"We've got to get away," she said. "I am sick to death of cities, books, and libraries. I want to find a place where there are no deadlines."

I nodded in agreement. "That would be great. We should do that sometime." The chief of geriatrics at the center had been pleased with our work and had already lined up our next project. I should have been honored. Instead, I was dreading it.

"I mean it, Bill. We've got to get out of New York, at least for a while."

"Where do you want to go?"

Jude shrugged her shoulders. It hurt me to see her so listless, so beaten down. She was right, of course. If we didn't do something, we'd be buried again in no time. Then it hit me. If we needed to get away, far away, we could go sailing.

"What do you say to renting a boat and spending a month in the Caribbean? It'll be just like the old days, only better."

She whirled around, her back now to the window, her face lit up. "That's it! It's just what we need." In that instant, her drive, her fire, and her passion came surging back.

"Let me deliver the manuscript," I told her, "and you start making some calls."

Jude's eyes were charged with excitement as she moved away from the window. "We could fly to San Juan and rent a sloop. Then we could sail south into the Lesser Antilles."

My own enthusiasm grew as I listened to her plans for our getaway. She was on the telephone making arrangements even before I was dressed and ready to make my delivery.

One week later, we were equipped, packed, and ready to go. I carried our few bags down to the sidewalk, and after a final inspection of the apartment, we closed the door, triple locked it, and walked away. We didn't know it, but that was the last time we would ever see the place we had called home for the last two years. Our carefully led, highly productive lives were about to collide with forces and events far beyond our understanding or control. Thankfully, we knew nothing of the storm that lay in our path.

Approaching Montserrat

THE WEATHER WAS GLORIOUS when we left San Juan and headed toward Montserrat. The 40-foot sloop that we had rented handled like a dream. The sea was gentle, and with Jude at the helm, the hull purred like a contented cat. Sitting on the deck, I knew that I loved our life at sea and, even more, that I loved Jude. She had been right; we really had needed to get away.

For months we had teetered between anger and exhaustion. Now the sun, water, and wind were washing away the grime that life and work in the city had deposited on us. I watched Jude at the helm, standing straight and tall and handling the boat with a lighter hand than mine. Our vacation was returning the shine to her skin and hair. I thought she had never looked more beautiful.

Suddenly I realized that although we had spent every waking minute together for the last two years, we had begun to drift apart. We had answered each other automatically with phrases like "I love you, too, honey . . ." that we had uttered without even looking up from what we were reading. Even our embraces had become absent-minded. Sure, we had worked together every day on something that we both loved, but it had been as if we were crawling down a long, dark tunnel together. All we could see and all we could think about was the speck of light in the distance. We had always faced forward; rarely had we faced each other. Month after month, we had been blind to the beauty of the world and each other. Our routine had been productive, but it had exacted a heavy price. For starters, I had let myself forget that marrying Jude was the best thing that had ever happened to me. I realized that Jude was the sun of my shadows, the light of my darkness. Before we go home, I told myself, we must promise to remember to take time out for vacations like this.

The morning we were to arrive in Montserrat, we were up with the sun. Below deck we spread out the navigation charts and double-checked our position. The wind had shifted 15 points to the north during the night and had strengthened slightly. We were sure we would make landfall by late afternoon. Our original calculations had called for us to arrive at Montserrat on

February 16, but the wind and weather had been flawless and we were a full day ahead of schedule. Also, the wind shift meant that we would be approaching the island from the east, which would give us the best view of the island's massive volcano. Jude said with a laugh that our little sloop had a magnetic attraction to Montserrat.

Jude saw the island first. Together, we watched the volcano grow from a faint purple hump on the horizon to a looming colossus of a mountain. It belched up a plume of smoke and ash that hovered like a halo around its peak. I remember the awe I felt at this sign of the volcano's ability to create and destroy. As the sun was setting, we decided to spend the night about three miles off shore. We turned into the wind and dropped a sea anchor.

And now my journal will tell you what happened.

Disaster

February something 1989 ∽

FATE HAS TURNED SAVAGELY against us. The betrayal stings doubly because we have lived so long with the illusion that we are immune to tragedy. Disaster, catastrophe, affliction . . . these things are visited upon other people. We only read about them in the morning paper.

Jude and I seethe with anger at this turn of fate, yet we dare not raise our voices above a whisper. Jude sits rigidly on one of the benches by the fire pit. I write in the journal supplied by the woman Hannah with our last meal. We each handle our fears in our own ways. Nothing like this was supposed to happen. Not to us.

People like us are not supposed to awaken in an unfamiliar dwelling, helpless and quivering with fear. Our bodies are not meant to be bruised and broken by forces we can neither see nor understand. The mantle of our good fortune was never supposed to be stripped violently from our shoulders.

Our ordeal began as we settled our sloop for the night in the shadow of Montserrat's stone giant. Jude had gone below deck to prepare supper. I stayed topside to take care of a few chores. Just as I was finishing, Jude called to me, saying that the galley stove would not light. I went below to see if I could help. It's a good thing I did.

We were together when the first rumble came. We didn't really hear it—the sound was too low for that. Instead, it rattled our bones. We stood stock-still. Neither of us spoke. We listened intently for several minutes but heard only our own irregular breathing. At last we relaxed and turned toward each other. I reached for her hand, and together we headed for the galley stairs.

Before we could reach them, another shock wave hit us. This one seemed a hundred times more powerful than the last. It threw us against the far wall of the galley. Jude slammed against the corner of a cabinet and cried out in pain. The sloop began to list badly to port. Water appeared from nowhere and gushed through the galley.

I waded to Jude's side and put her arm around my neck just as the third and most powerful shock ripped our sturdy little boat in two. The hull shrieked as it exploded around us. A blast of water from what had been the ceiling wrenched Jude's arm from my grip. I choked on the salty foam and fought against the surge that rapidly filled the galley. The stove hung at a crazy angle over my head, its oven door slamming open and closed like a huge taunting mouth. "Jude!" I tried to scream, but the rushing water stifled my voice. Sure that I was about to die, I struggled for one last gasp of air.

I cannot fully explain what happened next. Jude and I should have died in that place at that time. But we did not. Something reached out and wrapped itself around us. Something plucked us from the skeleton of that sinking ship. We were pulled down into water that was dark and very cold. The cold was numbing, the darkness terrifying. I struggled to break free but could not. I found myself remembering a childhood bully who had delighted in holding my head underwater. I remembered how I struggled against him. Most of all, I remembered the fear.

The pressure in my ears told me that I was far beneath the waves, and I was sure my next breath would fill my lungs with seawater. I was wracked by an unbearable agony. The icy water seemed determined to rip me apart. Unable to endure more, I gave in to the water, to whatever was pulling me down, and willed myself to let go. At the last possible instant, when I seemed to have reached the outermost limits of my endurance, the descent stopped, and I was shot toward the surface even more violently than I had been pulled under. A moment later, I found myself tumbling head over heels in the warm blue water of a large breaker rolling toward shore.

The wave broke and slammed me onto a hard sandy bottom with rock outcroppings. I felt a sharp pain in my shoulder. Then up on all fours, head raised out of the water, I gasped for three or four sweet, delicious breaths. There was just enough time to realize that Jude was beside me again before the undertow raced back from the shore and pulled us back into the sea. The next breaker dashed us against a huge rock that lay near the shore. Time and time again, we gasped for air and were drawn back into the sea.

Finally, a wave carried us far enough onto the shore that we were able to escape the pounding surf. We crawled as far away from the ocean as we could and collapsed onto the hard white sand.

Revival

J DON'T KNOW HOW LONG we lay unconscious on the beach, more dead than alive. When I woke up, Jude was beside me. Her breathing was soft and regular. We lay huddled in a warm bed that was round, smooth, and soft with a cupped center like a bird's nest. The night air was still, and the pale glow of the moon lit Jude's face. I rubbed my hand against my face. Several days' worth of stubble met my fingers.

Jude stirred and her eyes opened, "Are you all right?"

"I think so. How about you?"

She tried to turn onto her left side and moaned in pain. She rolled back to her original position.

"Where are we?" she whispered.

"I don't know," I whispered back, as if we were two children.

"This isn't a hospital," Jude continued. "It can't be a

19

hospital. It's so dark and we're in this bed—together."

"You're right," I sighed. "Maybe it's a village on Montserrat, or it's someone's house and they've taken us in."

"That can't be. There's no way we could be on Montserrat. It's impossible. We were miles from shore when we went down. And besides," Jude hesitated and turned her head away from me, "the beach was white. Montserrat's beaches have black sand."

In the silence that followed, we considered a gruesome thought. What if we had drowned in the wreck and were, in fact, dead? Was this some form of afterlife?

"I'm scared, Jude," I said. She reached out and found my hand. Neither of us spoke.

After a long while, I said, "I've gotta pee."

For some reason, this observation struck us as funny. It hurt terribly to laugh, but we laughed anyway.

Girding myself for the effort ahead, I shimmied to the side of the bed. I thought that it would be a struggle to climb over the edge, but it wasn't. The lip of the bed simply tipped closer to the ground. I sat up, turned, and put my feet on the floor. When I stood up, the bed rocked gently back to its neutral position.

On the floor directly in front of me, I found a small earthenware pot about a foot in diameter and six inches deep. It looked like a chamber pot. Given my growing sense of urgency, I figured it was one. I lifted the lid, relieved myself, and crawled back to the side of the bed feeling much better.

"I've never known a dead person," I told Jude, "but I'm willing to bet that dead people don't need to pee."

I helped her up so that she could make use of the facilities, and by the time we were both back in bed, our muscles trembled from the exertion. We could not speak. We simply slept.

We awoke again in the dark when a woman entered our quarters. She sat us up in bed and helped us each drink a cup of bitter tea. I remember little of what she said, but she spoke to us in English and her voice carried the delicate trace of a southern accent. Before she left, she promised to return in the morning.

We slept soundly, without dreaming, and awoke at dawn. At first we lay in bed, whispering our thoughts to each other, but as the minutes passed and the daylight gathered strength, we managed to sit up and examine our surroundings.

Standing like attendants around our bed were four large rose-colored urns. About three feet high, they tapered gently from the mouth to the base. A riot of flowers and herbs issued forth from each, filling the room with the subtle yet distinctive aroma of life and growth.

The urns stood on a floor that was a spectacular mosaic of tiny, brightly colored tiles. The tiles formed swirls that curled around and flowed through each other. If a dozen sunsets had been mixed together and brought indoors, it could not have been more beautiful.

The walls, by comparison, were rather plain. I judged the windowsills to be more than a foot thick. The windows themselves had no glass, and the morning breeze rustled the green curtains that hung by their sides. The walls appeared to have been built up by hand from innumerable layers of some kind of off-white plaster. They enclosed a single room that was quite small, probably no more than sixteen feet square.

The smoothness of the walls would have delighted us in our own home. The layer upon layer of plaster softened the angles and corners so that one wall seemed to blend into the next. Two east-facing windows filled the room with light. In the center were four low wooden benches, each about a foot high and two feet long. They surrounded a small fire pit made of dry laid stone. The only door was directly opposite our bed, on the far side of the room. It appeared to be fashioned from hand-hewn planks that had aged to a deep shade of brown. It hung from plain black hinges and fit snugly to its casing. Looking up, we saw a smoke hole in the ceiling above the fire pit. Clay pots filled with deep red, magnificently petaled flowers hung from the ceiling above our bed.

Jude whispered, "It's like being inside and outside at the same time."

We lay back, tired from the effort of sitting up. We could hear voices outside the room. They were in a tongue we couldn't understand. We listened carefully for even a single word that was familiar but heard none, although we could distinguish the voices of men, women, and children. There seemed to be the tinkle of wooden wind chimes in the breeze, adding their tones to those of the birds that we could hear singing.

The flood of sights and sounds was unsettling. We wondered, but dared not ask each other, who these people were and what they would do with us.

It was the aroma of food being cooked over an open fire that drove us from our bed. Getting up was painful. Our muscles and joints were not only bruised but stiff with disuse as well. Together, we leaned forward and, using each other for support, brought ourselves to a standing position. We held each other tight and thanked God that we were alive.

The sound of the front door opening pulled us apart. The woman from the night came into the room. This time, she brought a tray loaded with dishes of steaming food and two teapots.

In English, she invited us to sit down on the benches in the center of the room. With little prompting from our visitor, we began to eat. We shoveled down mouthful after mouthful of the delicious offerings, and when our plates were empty, she refilled them. As we ate, she told us the story of our arrival in this country.

"For three days before you came here, a great storm held us in its grasp. It came from the west, and not even the oldest soul among us can remember a storm with such great power. All of the trees bowed before the wind, and the rain came down like a river from the sky. We were frightened and did not dare stir from our homes. You can imagine our joy when the storm passed over the mountains."

She noticed that Jude's cup was empty and poured her another serving of the bitter tea. Bright red leaves floated in the bottom of our cups. Jude was thirsty and downed it quickly and without complaint.

The woman resumed her story. "Zachary, one of the boys from our village, was the first down to the shore after the storm broke. I'm afraid you gave him quite a scare when he came upon you. He thought you were dead. He ran back to the village, calling to us in full voice. We carried you here and laid you down in this bed. Few believed that you would survive the night. It is your good fortune that they were wrong."

We observed her closely as she spoke. She was a thin woman who stood perhaps five and a half feet tall. Her face bore the wrinkles that come with a lifetime of laughter and sunlight. Blue eyes sparkled at us as she spoke. Her thin lips curved into a smile easily, and a mane of brilliant white hair hung in a braid down her back. The most striking thing about her, though, was her dignity and poise. She moved and spoke with a quiet, unhurried confidence that made her easy to listen to—and to trust.

I noticed that her arms were well muscled for a woman of her age. She looked to be in her early seventies, though she clearly retained the better part of her youthful vigor.

The food and drink answered our hunger and thirst, but the act of consuming our meal left us immensely tired. The woman understood our fatigue and gently helped us back to bed. Then she drew a bench to the bedside and sat down.

"My name is Hannah. I will be watching over you as you regain your strength. In time, I will answer all of your questions, but now you must rest." She reached out and took Jude's hand in hers. "When you are stronger and the time is right, I will tell you about Kallimos."

We were too tired to think about what she was saying. Neither of us saw her rise or heard the door close behind her.

Kallimos

March? 1989 ~

STRENGTH IS CREEPING SLOWLY BACK into our muscles and our spirits. The more we look around the room, the more we are intrigued by this place. The craftsmanship that surrounds us speaks of the generations of artisans who have set their hands to work here. I have never known a room like this. It is both old and new. Its simplicity invites us to make it our own, yet we sense that it safeguards the secrets of ages long gone by. Still, our thoughts have turned increasingly to home and the people we have left behind. Our families must be sick with worry. I can only imagine their joy when they learn that we are safe.

We did not see Hannah again until the following morning, for we slept through the day and the night. In the morning, Hannah brought another abundant meal. We have enjoyed the food and, with her urging, continue to drink her distasteful tea.

While we were eating, Hannah asked us to tell her about the events that led to our arrival here. We told her about Montserrat's vengeful volcano. She shuddered visibly as we gave our account of being sucked from the ship's broken hull. We told her how we had been slammed against the shore and of our struggle to escape the undertow. When we were finished, we were exhausted but able to return to bed unassisted. We slept.

This evening, Hannah set before us another feast and what seemed to be a gallon of her tea. Our appetites are strong and growing, as is our desire to go home. When we raised the subject of returning home, however, Hannah's face clouded over. Trembling slightly, she looked away and hesitated before she spoke. "I came here just as you did, but a very long time ago. I was just a child when they found me washed up on this shore. The people of the village took me in, nursed me back to health, and welcomed me into their world. They will do the same for you."

Her remarks puzzled us. We had found Hannah to be more straightforward than this. "That's great, Hannah," I replied. "You seem to have found health and happiness, but we have no desire to remain here. Don't take this the wrong way. We're very grateful for all you've done, but we need to go home. We're strong enough to travel now, and we'd appreciate some help getting on our way."

Hannah leaned forward and set her chin in her hands. Her voice dropped almost to a whisper. "I don't know how to tell you this. I doubt you will believe me when you hear the truth about your situation." The change in her manner set Jude and me on edge. "No one knows how or why it happens, but on very rare occasions strangers appear on the shore of Kallimos. People say the strangers come from the Other World. I, like you, came here from the Other World. I was just nine years old when I arrived. My father was a physician, and we lived in Norfolk, Virginia. He was a skillful sailor and he loved the sea. Each winter, we took our holiday among the islands of the Caribbean. Our boat was destroyed as yours was, and the cold, dark water you describe pulled me from my mother's arms."

Tears welled in Hannah's eyes. She paused for a moment and then continued. "A woman named Haleigh, whom you will meet, took me in and raised me. She helped me grieve for my lost life and the death of my parents. Being with you reminds me of the life I lost that day. But since the days of the ancients, no one from the Other World has ever returned to it. There is no way back. Kallimos is your world now; you will spend the rest of your lives here."

Anger and fear raced through me. I fought to control my voice. "Well, that's quite a story. But surely you don't expect us to believe it, do you? I mean, you've been won-

28

derful, but just get us to a phone and I'll make all the necessary arrangements."

Hannah bit her lip and raised her head to stare at the mountains that stood blue and distant outside our windows. My self-control began to crumble in the silence, and I raised my voice. "Listen, ma'am, you cannot seriously believe that we are going to buy this 'land that time forgot' scenario. Our boat went down at 62 degrees 5 minutes west longitude and 16 degrees 35 minutes north latitude. We are somewhere near there right now, and we just want to go home."

The obvious anger in my voice led Jude to shift apprehensively on her bench. Hannah didn't move an inch. "I know the pain and the fear that grip you. You have been given a heavy burden. Still, you must accept that the life you led in the Other World is gone. Kallimos is your home now."

I leaped up from my seat and yelled at her, "Look, I don't know if this is some kind of tropical loony bin or what, but you are a crazy old woman and we are going home!" I jabbed my finger toward her face.

Somehow, she remained unperturbed. "The pain of your loss is great. But I can assure you that, in time, you will know the ways of the people of Kallimos and become part of this world. Fate has given you this life, both of you. Now you both must learn how to live it."

I am ashamed to record what happened next. I shrieked at her in a mindless rage and kicked over the bench on which I had been sitting. I stormed around the room, shouting, "We are citizens of the United States, and we have rights. Do you know the penalties for kidnapping? Do you want to spend the rest of your life in prison? If you value your life, you will take us to the United States embassy and you will take us there now!" Outside, the voices we heard every day were silent; even the birds had stopped singing. The violence of my outburst had filled the little cottage, spilled out its windows, and now hung in the air around us like some deathly fog.

Hannah spoke to me again, her voice as soft and gentle as ever. "When I first came to Kallimos, I cried for my mother every night. Haleigh held me. She rocked me and sang to me. Haleigh taught me the ways of Kallimos. It will take some time for both of you, but you will grow to love this world. Kallimos is your home now. You must learn its ways. Do not be afraid. There are many here who will help you."

A gentle rain began to spatter against the roof.

"Tomorrow we will begin." With these words, Hannah gathered her belongings and stood up. We watched as she stepped out of our cottage and into the softly falling rain. After her departure, Jude and I held each other tight and cried until there were no more tears left.

Jude has been asleep for probably two hours now. I'm finally ready to crawl into bed and hope that this is just a dream.

Welcome

Still March? 1989 ~

WE AWOKE THIS MORNING to the soft sounds of Kallimos, sounds that, if Hannah is right, we will come to know very well. Hannah appeared in our room, as she has every day, shortly after we awoke. Today, however, she provided a wash basin and soap, and she discreetly looked away as we washed ourselves. It felt so good to be clean again!

Then we noticed that Hannah was placing fresh, clean clothes for each of us on the bed. Her face beamed with anticipation, making it clear that yesterday's outburst had been forgiven.

The clothes worn here are simple but quite beautiful. Ours have been cut from a tightly woven cloth with repeating patterns of color and shape. Shades of blue and green are woven one into another in a fashion I have never seen before. To the touch, the fabric resembles cotton but without the machined uniformity of the cotton we know. Each outfit consists of a tunic cut loosely to allow for freedom of movement, a pair of trousers constructed of a heavier material, though not as heavy as denim, and a colorful cloth belt that can be tied at the waist. Leather-soled sandals complete our attire. Except for their size, and the patterns worked into the material, there seems to be no difference between the clothes offered to Jude and those offered to me. Hannah says that the people of Kallimos do not distinguish between clothing worn by men and by women. Like us, she had thought this odd at first, she said, but with time, it seemed to make perfect sense.

I have to admit I felt foolish as I dressed. I have always felt most comfortable in a sport coat and tie. I blushed at the thought of traipsing about in clothes that seemed best suited to the denizens of Haight-Ashbury circa 1968.

After complimenting us on our appearance and offering some gentle words of encouragement, Hannah led us out of our cottage for the first time. Upon stepping through the door, we saw that our room is actually a small cottage with a front porch that overlooks an egg-shaped village green. The green is perhaps a hundred yards long and, at its widest point, maybe fifty yards across. It is ringed by thirty to forty small stone cottages much like our own. A fire pit and tripod dominate the center of the green. We could see steam rising from a great black cauldron that hung over the fire, and an unusual scent hung in the air.

"Today is the day the village makes soap," Hannah explained as we stared at the green.

Hannah then put her arms around our waists and whispered that we should walk with her to the center of the green. There were perhaps two dozen people standing and sitting right near the fire, mostly in groups of four or five. Others watched us from their porches. In all, there were seventy to eighty people on or around the green. They observed us closely but remained silent until Hannah began to speak in their language. Her words quickly melted their reserve. Smiles and friendly nods spread among them. Words of welcome, which we did not understand, followed quickly. Children, who had hidden behind their mothers, peeked out at us.

Before she left us this evening, I asked Hannah how she had introduced us. She said, "I told the people that the rumors were true, that you two really were from the Other World, and I told them to welcome you. I also told them not to be afraid of you. I said, 'Do not fear the man's loud words, for inside he is a frightened boy. Your gentleness will soothe his troubled spirit.'"

With these simple words, we entered the world of Kallimos. Every member of the village came to our side. They smiled and laid their hands upon us. Everyone who could touched us. Those who couldn't touch us directly put a hand on someone who was touching us. Gradually, a circle formed around us. When the circle was complete, Hannah led a chant. The chant, which was repeated ten times, had a melody that I found very soothing. It was almost like a lullaby. According to Hannah, the chant in English would go as follows:

I give to you,
From you I receive.
Together we turn,
And plant the seed.

After the chant, the people of the village raised a loud, welcoming cheer that dissolved into laughter. With simple gestures and nods, they invited us to eat our first meal in their company. We can only guess at what they asked us and what they said about us.

Reflection

$\mathcal{J}$ STILL FEEL LOST. My efforts to think clearly about our current situation have born little fruit because I am never really sure where to begin. By all that's logical, we should be somewhere near Montserrat, but every morning I look out my window at a range of snow-capped mountains. There are no mountains like these in the Caribbean basin. No matter how hard I try, I cannot make sense of our situation.

All the evidence points to the fact that Jude and I have been deposited in some remote, undiscovered corner of the world. I have no idea how this could have happened or even where on Earth we are. Not surprisingly, I have no idea how we will ever get back home. In fact, so far, I have found no reason to doubt Hannah's assertion that we are stranded here forever.

Our bruises faded from their first angry purple to a pale yellow and are now gone. Our torn muscles have mended. Each day brings us more strength and less pain. Even my shoulder, which had been quite tender, feels better. Each day, we spend more time talking, listening, and exploring our environment and less time resting and sleeping. No effort has been made to restrain us. Thus, Jude and I have conducted daily explorations of the surrounding area. We hoped at first to stumble upon some undiscovered passage that would lead us back home.

Our reconnaissance has revealed that the village lies on a narrow strip of gradually rising ground about a quarter of a mile east of the beach and perhaps thirty to forty feet above sea level. The village is guarded on this side by a grove of ancient trees whose trunks are so large that, at their base, neither Jude nor I can reach our arms around them. Their bark is a rich brown and smells vaguely of coffee. Their limbs are hung with broad, fan-shaped leaves that are dark green on one side with disorderly red-yellow patterns on the other. To see them flutter in the breeze is a delightful spectacle.

Just to the west of the village the land rises. The people of the village call these the Summer Hills and, for as long as anyone can remember, their meadows have been used to pasture the village livestock. Far to the south and east, are the Pal-Chin mountains. These are the peaks we see from our cottage windows. Hannah says that beyond them to the east lies a great desert, though she admits that no one from the village has ever been there.

Just south of the village is a vast—at least, they say it's vast—woodland known as Caleb's Forest. A long series of ridges and valleys is said to be carved into the earth there. Little is known of what lies beyond the forest other than mountains. Just beyond the northern edge of the village is the commonly held garden. We were surprised to learn that it is only two acres in size. It seems too small to feed the village, but somehow it does. When we hiked north past the garden, we came across a river that was too wide and too deep to cross on our own. The water flowed swiftly and felt very cold. Hannah calls it the Kwa-Na-Na River and says that its source is in the mountains. Beyond the river is said to be wilderness.

It seems that we are trapped here. Certainly there is no easy way out and no place to go if we left the village. Jude and I are certain that our families have held our funerals by now. They mourn beside empty graves. Still, our lot could be much worse. Robinson Crusoe spent thirty savage years living alone on an island. We, at least, have each other.

I've lost track of time. My best guess is that a month has passed since our arrival here. In that time, the people of Kallimos have welcomed us into their hearts and their community. They have fed and sheltered our bodies and tended to our wounded spirits. They make us feel safe, and that is important because loneliness for our families, for our way of life, and a fear of the future still darken our hearts. It is our curse that fate tore us from the lives we had made for ourselves. It may be our blessing that we have come to Kallimos.

The First Lesson

March? April? 1989 ～

THIS MORNING, HANNAH INVITED US to join her for supper. This will be our first "night out" since our arrival in Kallimos, and we relish the thought of it. The calm of evening is spreading across the village as I write. Jude is getting herself ready and bemoaning the lack of a mirror. For my part, I have grown accustomed to my now full beard. There are no razors here. I think Jude likes it, though I can't get her to say so. Hannah's home is cater-corner across the green from our own, less than a hundred yards away. All of the houses in the village are within a couple minutes' walk of each other. Jude's ready, so it's time to go. More later.

Just got back from dinner with Hannah, and I am compelled to write while our talk is still fresh in my mind. Hannah's home, like ours, is a one-story cottage with an inviting front porch and one sparsely furnished room. In the fashion of all the homes here, the walls are thick, and vegetation hangs around the place like a fragrant, living curtain.

Jude and I tingled with excitement as we made our way there. We stepped onto the porch, knocked on her door, and were greeted with a smile as Hannah swung the door open. The scent of flowers and spices billowed out from the cottage. Hannah invited us to sit down on the benches that surrounded the fire pit. Our timing was perfect, she said, because she had just started to prepare our meal. According to Hannah, the people of Kallimos regard the preparation of a meal to be part of the meal itself. We talked casually as she conjured a feast of spicy roast peppers and rice from her simple provisions. I have never eaten better food. Our dessert was a small bottle of sweet, fruity wine.

"I've found so much pleasure in your healing," Hannah said, as we sipped our wine. "Death could easily have claimed you both. I am happy that you were able to turn him away." Her face glowed in the candlelight.

"Now that you are stronger, the time has come for us to learn more about each other. You two young people are the first to have come here from the Other World since my arrival. The people have ancient stories about the Other World, but those tales are rarely told, and since my first few years here, I have seldom found cause to think of my beginnings there. Woodrow Wilson was president when my parents and I went sailing. My father had just purchased an automobile. He was so proud of that thing. I think he called it a Model Z. He used it to drive us to the marina the day we left for our cruise. That was so long ago."

Hannah looked away from us and into the fire. After a long moment, she shook her head and lifted her gaze, ready for a new topic. "As you know, Haleigh showed me the ways of the people here. She taught me the names of all the herbs and flowers that grow in our forests and meadows. She told me the stories and legends of the people. When I became a woman, she showed me how to combine these things to heal the sick and the injured."

"So, then, you're the village doctor?" I asked.

"Well, the people wouldn't say 'doctor.' The word they use is something more like 'guide' or 'healing guide.' It is strange if you think about it. If I had stayed in the Other World, I would surely have married and raised a family. By leaving that world, I was able to follow my father's example and become a healer."

Jude said, "So that's why you're the one who has tended to us. You have been guiding us back to health."

Hannah allowed that this was so and went on to tell us about the families of the village. She knows everyone and has an encyclopedic knowledge of their histories

42

and the relationships that bind them one to another. The cottage next to ours is inhabited by Zachary and his father—Zachary was the young boy who found us on the beach. We learned that his father is a carpenter and a roofer and that his mother died from a spider bite just six summers ago. Haleigh tends the village garden and did so even before Hannah's arrival.

We listened intently and marveled at this woman. Judging from what she recalls of her life before she arrived in Kallimos, she is older than I first thought, probably in her eighties rather than her seventies. She knows everything about the village but nothing of the Great Depression, World War II, the atom bomb, the Cold War, Vietnam, Woodstock, or the rise and fall of the Soviet Union. She did not know, until we told her, that men have walked on the moon, the same moon that now peered in at us through the open window.

When the last inhabitant had been described, Hannah said, "That is my story. Now tell me yours. Tell me of the lives you led in the Other World."

With that invitation, Jude and I began to talk about how we met and the work we did together. We went on at great length and concluded with the rather boastful claim that we knew more about the aging human being than any other two people on Earth. Hannah looked excited and asked us to go on. She said that she was eager to learn more.

I plunged into a discussion of cellular immunity in aging human tissues. Jude threw in corrections and explanations along the way.

When we finished, Hannah smiled and said, "My heavens! I have no idea what you two are talking about, but I'm afraid you understand far less about elders than you think you do."

We were stunned.

Hannah continued, "You are young and brave and you have learned much, but you have so very far to go. You seem to understand so many little things but none of the big things. If you would like, we can teach you the true nature of elders."

"Well, sure, Hannah, we're young," I shot back, "but we've spent years studying these issues. We've been given access to the most advanced research available. Some of it hadn't even been published when we reviewed it. No two people on Earth know the aging process as well as we do."

"Maybe that's so," Hannah said, "but tell me what you know of the three plagues of the elders."

Jude and I looked at each other. Our minds raced through the research we had read. We wanted so much to impress Hannah with our skill and knowledge. Finally, Jude ventured, "Memory loss, arthritis, and stroke?"

Hannah shook her head. "For longer than anyone can remember, the people of Kallimos have understood and taught their young about the three plagues—loneliness, helplessness, and boredom. The stories of the people teach us that we must help our elders defend themselves from these afflictions."

"Come on, that was a trick question," I said. "Those things aren't plagues. They aren't even diseases. Anyone can be lonely or bored. What makes loneliness, boredom, and, and . . ."

Jude chimed in, "Helplessness."

"Fine. Helplessness. What makes those things special to the geriatric population?"

"By 'geriatric population' I suppose you mean our elders," Hannah responded. "I am concerned that your heads are filled with snarls and tangles. You rejoice in complicated details and you fiddle with elaborate puzzles, but you still don't know what it means to grow old."

"You're not being fair, Hannah," I argued. "I realize it's not your fault, but you never had a complete education. If you had, you would understand how important these details are."

"Well, then, this really is my chance to learn, isn't it?" She had an almost playful look on her face.

I smiled broadly. "That's right! Jude and I couldn't be happier than to teach you. It's the least we can do. After all, you did save our lives."

"There is one thing I have been wondering, and perhaps you can help me," Hannah said.

"Go ahead."

"Tell me, why do elders exist?"

Jude furrowed her brow. "Why do they exist?"

"Yes, tell me why."

This was a new question for us. We had always taken the presence of older adults for granted.

"All living things decline with advancing age," I said uncertainly, trying to feel my way toward an answer. "People are born, they mature, and they get old. That's the way life is."

"The living creatures of this world get older everyday, that's true enough," Hannah replied. "But in the long history of this good Earth, only human beings have protected their elderly from harm. For all other creatures, death follows hard on the heels of decline."

We considered Hannah's words carefully. Slowly it dawned on us that she was right.

"I see what you mean," Jude said thoughtfully. "There is a difference between becoming old and becoming elderly. Becoming old is a universal reality of biology; becoming elderly requires protection by others."

I picked up where Jude left off. "Do you realize what you are saying, Hannah? By your standard, an elder is one who relies on the support and protection of the village for survival. Thus, an elder, by definition, is a burden on the community. Is this any way to think of the

46

elderly? Who could ever look forward to becoming a burden on their community?"

Hannah chose her words carefully. "You think only of what the village bestows upon the elder, and you forget that the elder returns a much more valuable gift to the village."

Jude said, "Bill and I have seen the elders playing with the children, if that's what you mean."

I added, "I'm sure they're a repository for traditions, folktales, myths, and the like."

"Yes, the elders do serve the village in those ways," Hannah replied. "It is true that by the community coming together and protecting elders from the plagues of loneliness, helplessness, and boredom, the elders are given the opportunity to pass on to the community their experience, their wisdom, their knowledge of life. Thus, the community helps the elders and the elders help the community. Still, the people of Kallimos hold their greatest reverence for what the most fragile elders give. Elders who can no longer speak and no longer walk give the greatest gift of all."

I was totally lost. I held up my hands as if pleading for mercy. "All right, I surrender. I surrender, and I apologize for the way I talked down to you earlier. I can't even guess where you are going from here. The truth is that I've never thought about aging in this way. What is the gift? Why do elders exist?"

Hannah smiled gently, "Elders exist because they teach us how to make a community. As we give to them, they give to us their wisdom, their experience, their affection. When we come together to meet their needs, we learn how to live as human beings. They instruct us in the art of caring. There is no more precious a gift than that. The best communities are those most willing to pick up and carry the burdens of their frailest elders."

Jude leaned back and breathed a deep sigh. "So that's it," she said. "That's why this place feels so different from home. This village has wrapped itself around its elders. Serving them has given you gentleness and patience."

I thought about the world we had left behind, and a wave of disgust rose inside of me. Suddenly, I realized that our society is organized around the skills, capacities, and needs of mature, able-bodied adults. It is their necessities, their wants, and their desires that shape our world. All of the programs and services, all of the agencies and institutions I had so carefully studied miss the point. They work relentlessly to assure that the elderly conform to their requirements. Never do they ask how society can be adjusted to the needs of the elderly. They have been designed to discharge our obligation to the elderly efficiently and effectively. We provide charitably for our elders; we do not center our communities around them.

"I understand," were the only words I could bring myself to say.

"Will you tell us more about the three plagues?" Jude asked.

Hannah responded, "Through their words and their deeds, our elders teach us that *dohavkee*—'belonging' or 'oneness' might be the best term in English—lies at the heart of a life worth living. We know that, from the very first moment of life, the human being seeks connections, *havkees*. The first task of the child growing inside its mother is to connect itself to the womb. The umbilical cord is our first link to the world beyond ourselves. When a baby is born and the cord is cut, the baby immediately seeks its mother's breast. So it goes for the whole of a human life.

"But as many seasons pass, time does its work. The strength needed to draw water from a well slips away. The work of gathering herbs and nuts for meals becomes a burden. Slowly but surely, death steals away those whom the elder has loved long and well. As each *havkeen* breaks, the elder is loosened from his or her place among us. Loneliness seeps in where once it was held at bay. Helplessness slithers into the heart, into this elder who has done so much for so many! At last, boredom invades and conquers the spirit. The long, empty hours become like a stone on the chest. The three plagues are deadly, and no work is more sacred than defending our elders against them."

We sat motionless and humbled. The light from the dying fire flickered across Hannah's face. The village lay silent in the night.

"I don't understand why you have been brought here," Hannah finally said. "I do know that when you come to understand our elders, you will understand us. The people of Kallimos have built their world on simple ideas of great power. You must seek out these principles, master them, and strive to live by them. If you do these things, you will make for yourselves a life worth living."

Hannah rose from her place; the conversation was over. Jude and I thanked her and said that we hoped she would continue to visit us. We did not speak as we crossed the village green. Once inside our cottage, I lit a candle and pulled out my journal. Jude stood frowning in front of the fire. "I feel like a fool," she said. "I have poured my heart and soul into understanding how we can help the elderly fit into society and have never given a single thought to the idea of making society fit the elderly. It's so simple once you see it—when we defend the elderly from loneliness, helplessness, and boredom, our lives and their lives are better."

I slammed my journal down on the bench.

"What's the matter?"

"I can't believe one little question could blow such a huge hole in our work."

"There's nothing we can do about it now," Jude said gently.

I grunted in response. I did not like to be reminded that we were stranded here. "The other thing that gets me is Hannah's claim that our future happiness here depends on our discovering the 'simple ideas' that govern life in Kallimos. Why doesn't she just come out and tell us what they are?"

Jude had already crawled into bed. "I don't think that's the way things work here," she answered drowsily.

The candle is almost gone, and it is very late. If we must learn for ourselves the simple ideas of Kallimos, perhaps we were introduced to the first one tonight. I am going to put it this way:

> The three plagues of loneliness, helplessness, and boredom account for the bulk of suffering in a human community.

The People

LAST NIGHT, I HEARD MY MOTHER'S VOICE in a dream. She stood at the back door of my childhood home and called to me. The sound of my name carried easily across the crisp air of the autumn afternoon. I raced home, fallen leaves scattering as I ran. Inside, the warm scent of potatoes and meat greeted me. As daylight slipped away, I ate the supper she had prepared, and I listened to the wind clattering against the bare trees outside the window. Mother listened to my prayers, gave me a kiss, and turned out the light. Though I was alone, I was unafraid.

When I awoke, I was again on Kallimos. I closed my eyes and, for the thousandth time, relived the shipwreck. I can find no reason why this has happened to us. My body has healed, but the gash this experience has torn in my life remains an open wound. My heart aches. I want to go home.

Two weeks have passed since our dinner with Hannah. I know this, for every morning since that night, I have placed a pebble on the windowsill. Two piles of seven greeted me this morning. Little has changed in that time.

We have mastered perhaps a half dozen phrases of the people's language, so we can now exchange pleasantries with those we meet. We know we must learn more of the language and the ways of these people. I think it will be a pleasant if simple task. Everything we have seen and heard tells us that these are kind-hearted people who reckon time in moons and seasons rather than days. My instincts tell me that discord, striving, and hate are customary in any human life. Still, there seems to be a depth of peacefulness here that goes far beyond a simple absence of strife.

We eat our breakfast with the people every morning and then retreat to our front porch to watch the life of the village unfold before us as we try to discover the source of this peacefulness. It is a life that proceeds at a painfully slow pace. Eating, cooking, baking, cleaning, over and over again, the same people doing the same things in the same place, day after day after day. I can now fully appreciate Marx's thoughts about the idiocy of rural life. There is nothing new here. I miss the intensity, the jostling, and the anxiety that drove our lives before the wreck. People here conduct themselves as if they have endless amounts of time. They don't seem to worry about anything, and that worries me. If we are going to spend the rest of our lives here, we will have to lower our expectations a long way. I am not sure that we can or should settle for so little. Hannah may love this life, but she came here as a child. We have no such saving grace. Jude and I can already feel boredom approaching. I fear that it will soon overtake us.

Three days ago, Jude gave me a new perspective on the village and its people. It was the middle of the afternoon, and we were on our porch, shunning the midday heat. Our lazy, meandering conversation finally turned to a subject that troubled us both. We were supposed to be experts in human psychology and behavior, but neither of us had been able to unearth the foundations upon which life in Kallimos was built. I was ready to give up on the whole effort, but Jude persuaded me to give it one more try.

"What do you see," she asked, "when you watch these people?" I hesitated for a moment and then decided to be blunt. "They are a primitive people who devote themselves to subsistence level agriculture and handicrafts. Singing, chanting, and storytelling fill the remainder of their hours. It's very simple, very dull, and we're stuck here."

Jude was ready with a thought. "There, that's it. That's the problem. You're doing it, and I'm doing it, too."

"Doing what?" I asked.

"We've been watching them, judging them, evaluating them by our own other-world yardstick. We compare them to New Yorkers and find them lacking. We've been caught up in all the things they aren't, and we've never gotten around to searching for what they are."

I sighed, certain that this discussion, like all the others, was going nowhere. "Get real, Jude," I said. "You can't say that this is our problem. What can be said in defense of a culture so completely lacking in initiative, curiosity, and progress? This place is a dead end."

"I think you're wrong."

"You just don't want to face up to all the things that are missing here. There are no telephones, no electricity, no pumps, no refrigeration, no vehicles of any kind. Drudgery has crushed these people so completely that they never will produce any of those things."

"But what about the things that are here?" Jude insisted. "You know, the things we got a glimpse of when we had dinner with Hannah. You'd see them if you took off your blinders and really looked." Jude's quiet voice shook with a passion that surprised us both.

I backed down. "What have you seen, Jude?"

She hesitated for a moment, as if embarrassed by

what she was about to say. "These people have raised caring for one another to the same kind of high art form that we have raised machines and technology."

I thought about her statement, and the more I thought, the more I saw how it might be true. I asked her to go on.

"We haven't seen it because we haven't looked for it," Jude said. "Think about it. Their technology is primitive, but they're always ready for a laugh, a song, or a story. They provide themselves with the simplest of food, clothing, shelter, yet they lavish attention and affection on each other. They act as if finding joy in one another is an end in itself rather than a means to something else."

I could feel the blood rise in my neck and fill my face. "We couldn't see it," I said reluctantly, "because we've never lived that way. We've put so much of our faith into science and technology that we've had precious little for other people."

"Measured against conventional standards, the village is impoverished and woefully underdeveloped, but . . ."

I interrupted her, "There is another kind of wealth here." Something stirred deep inside me. "I wonder," I asked, "what would it be like to belong here?"

Lost in her own thoughts, Jude didn't answer. In the silence that followed, the pulse of excitement, the wonderful sense of possibility that had moved me, faded away. The moment passed, and my doubts about Kallimos returned with full force.

We have continued to study the comings and goings around us with a new vitality. I have conducted an unofficial census and determined that, counting Jude and myself, seventy-four people live in this village.

Here's a simple but important difference between Kallimos and the rest of the world: The people here do not segregate age groups as we do. Hannah says they don't celebrate birthdays or even reckon age in terms of years. From our front porch, we see babes in arms and wizened old men and women interacting. Two older, clearly demented women are welcomed freely and easily into daily life.

The role of children remains somewhat puzzling. Some might say that there are no children here, or at least no childhood in our sense of the word. We naturally think of childhood as a time in which the young are shielded from the rough and tumble of adult life. They are catered to and allowed to be a breed apart. Here, on the other hand, the people weave their young seamlessly into the daily life of the village. The young play, work, laugh, learn, and sing along with the rest of the people.

There does seem to be a special bond between the elders and the young. Elders take time to play with, sing with, and tell stories to the children. In fact, the relationship between the elders and the children seems to account for the whole of their education. Despite our careful inspection of the village, we have yet to see any sign of a school. It seems that no one has special responsibility for teaching the children because everyone is responsible. This afternoon, we shared our observations with Hannah. We sat under a sprawling shade tree near the edge of the village green and excitedly compared and contrasted life as it is lived here and back home. When we had finished, Hannah sighed heavily and leaned back against the trunk of the tree. She was silent for several minutes.

"The stories you just told me of the powerful machines that have conquered the lives of human beings in the Other World sadden me. In the years since I came here, I have had little reason to consider the Other World and what life is like there." She paused for a moment before continuing. "You are seeing the people of Kallimos with strangers' eyes. I have not seen them or thought about them in that way since I was a child. As a child, I wondered if I had been delivered into the Garden of Eden."

Jude and I looked at each other with alarm. Hannah's words had reawakened our anxieties. Was Kallimos indeed some form of spiritual afterlife?

Hannah smiled, "I can assure you that this is not the Garden of Eden. We know death here. We are fully aware of the difference between good and evil, and we struggle with that difference, as all humans must."

We laughed nervously. It is embarrassing how easily Hannah intuits our thinking.

"My mother used to read stories to me at bedtime. I remember one called 'The Tortoise and the Hare.' You remind me of the animals who thought the tortoise would lose. They could not see his virtue, only the hare's quickness. Each of us works hard in our own way. We strive to succeed." Her eyes twinkled for a brief moment, "We even jostle one another on occasion. But the people of Kallimos remember and live by a lesson that the Other World forgot long ago. Here we know that human beings are meant to live in a garden, and we arrange our lives accordingly."

Hannah's words seemed far too simple to me. I didn't think that our lives and our world could be dismissed that easily. "You're really sweet," I said to her, "but there

59

is so much you don't understand. You've been here for so long that you've lost your sense of perspective. You simply can't see beyond this little village. Life here is pleasant, but it could be better, better even than the life you lived before you came here."

Jude shifted nervously next to me as I went on. "Just face a few facts, Hannah. This village has barely made it out of the Stone Age. Everything about this place is dull and stunted. At home, I have thousands of life-saving drugs at my disposal; you have to make do with handfuls of roots and leaves. Back home, I can communicate with people all over the globe like this," I snapped my fingers. "You can't even post a letter to the next village east of here." With that, Jude grabbed my arm and shot me a look that said, STOP. I stopped.

It was quiet except for the children and the elders, who were talking together on the other side of the green.

Hannah shook her head slowly. "Some of what you say is true, but there is a much larger truth that you ignore. You have medicines that I lack, but you have admitted that your elders suffer terribly from the three plagues. What good are your drugs for an elder dying of a broken heart? Your words can circle the Earth, but what good is that when you live for years without learning your neighbors' names? You hug your science and your machines as we hug our children, our elders, our neighbors. But do they hug you?"

She pointed to a patch of exuberant, lemon-colored flowers that sprang from their stalks like upturned bells. "Look at those flowers," she said. The flowers crowded around us like a flock of hungry chickens. "They are meant to live in the moist, shady soil that surrounds great trees like this one. Only a fool would plant them in the open or in dry soil. Though they are often tempted to forget it, human beings are much like these flowers. We are meant to live in a world that revolves around plants, animals, and children. So it has been since human beings first walked this Earth, and so it will always be. Your machines and your science will never change this."

Jude spoke up. "At home, most people consider plants, animals, and children to be pleasant distractions from the real business of living. Millions of people have pets, millions more enjoy gardening, and almost every neighborhood has a park or playground where you can watch children play. But what you're saying, I think, is that these things should be at the center of our lives, that we need to change the focus."

Hannah nodded in appreciation of Jude's comment and then changed the subject. "I asked you to meet me here today because the time has come for you to take your place among the people of the village."

"What do you mean?" Jude asked.

"Your healing is complete. It is time for you to begin

your work here. The people of the village have support-
ed you in your healing, and now it is time for you to give
back to the village."

Eager to make up for my earlier harsh words, I
jumped right in. "I'd be happy to serve as the physician
for the village," I offered. "It's the least I can do."

"Your offer is very kind, but I'm afraid we have no
such need," Hannah replied. "After all, as you yourself
have said, our medical treatments are limited to a number of herbal remedies, and you know nothing about
their proper uses."

She really did have me there. "Well, maybe I could
do research of some kind," I replied. "I could set up clinical trials to test some of your herbs and identify the
active compounds and then extract the . . ."

Hannah held up her hand. "Again, your offer is very
generous, but what we need is a new goatherd."

"A goatherd?" I repeated. "You've got to be kidding."
Jude burst out laughing. I glared at her.

"I don't know one blessed thing about goats," I
protested. "You're being ridiculous."

Hannah remained unmoved. "We need a goatherd,
and we believe that you will do a fine job."

I sat back, too stunned to argue any further. All I
could think was that I had graduated from Harvard, and
these people saw me as a potential goatherd.

Hannah turned her attention to Jude. "My dear,

Haleigh needs an extra pair of hands in the village garden, and we think you would do quite well there."

"It would be an honor," Jude said. "I've always wanted to learn to garden. Will Haleigh teach me?"

"She will teach you about much more than the garden," Hannah told her. "You can be sure of that."

Hannah groaned softly as she pulled herself up and brushed herself off. "I must go now," she told us. Turning to me, she added, "I will come for you in the morning and get you started with the goats." To Jude, she said, "Haleigh will be expecting you in the morning as well."

So here I am on the night before we begin our new careers, with a thin crescent moon peeking through our window, trying to keep my journal up to date. I should have gone to bed hours ago. At any rate, it seems clear that in addition to offering us her own special brand of vocational counseling this afternoon, Hannah was intent on teaching us something else. I'm not sure I understand it enough to put it into words just now. Maybe sleeping on it will help.

A Goatherd

I'VE STOPPED COUNTING THE DAYS. I've abandoned my stone calendar without regret. Two full moons have come and gone since my last entry; it is high summer now. I have become the people's goatherd and, for the first time in my life, I know contentment. I know in my heart now what Hannah was trying to teach us in that conversation:

> Life in a truly human community revolves around
> close and continuing contact with children, plants, and
> animals. These ancient relationships provide young
> and old alike with a pathway to a life worth living.

My peace of mind has not been gained easily. My vanity was deeply wounded when Hannah told me that I was going to be tending to livestock. Given my earlier outbursts on the backwardness of Kallimos, I was sure

64

this was her revenge. I felt strongly that it was jealousy on Hannah's part that kept me from serving as village physician. It was only Jude's soothing words that kept me from venting my anger at Hannah fully and publicly. Her loving counsel finally convinced me to stow my paranoia and assume the role assigned to me.

Was there ever a rawer recruit? The fog was just beginning to lift when Hannah met me at our door that first morning. As we walked to the goat barn at the west edge of the village, she outlined for me a typical day in the life of a goatherd. In the early morning, she explained, the goats are let out of the barn onto the trail that climbs away from the village and into the Summer Hills. The village goatherd is supposed to follow them along this winding path until they reach the high meadows. These meadows have been in continuous use by the people of the village since ancient times, and in addition to tending to the goats, it is the job of the goatherd to protect the grass from overgrazing. The goats must be moved before damage is done.

When we reached the meadows, Hannah taught me how to tell that a pasture is wearing thin. She also cautioned me against letting any goat wander away from the herd. A watchful eye is necessary, she said, to ensure that they all return safely to the barn. When I asked her if it wouldn't be more efficient to just fence them in, she gave me a puzzled look. "If we did that, what would the goatherd do?" she asked. Since I didn't have an answer, she finished her job description. When the sun begins to weaken, the goatherd turns the herd toward home. Once the barn is reached, he whistles for the children and elders who assist with the milking. After the goats are watered and bedded down, the goatherd's work is done.

The tasks were simple enough, I discovered, but the idea that this was now my vocation continued to gall me. It took every bit of Jude's coaxing to get me out of bed at first. With no one to talk to and nothing to do but watch the goats and grass, I spent weeks concocting elaborate arguments that proved beyond any doubt that goatherding was a tremendous waste of my time, talents, and energies. It is surprising just how toxic a brew loneliness and self-pity can make.

When I first began stopping by Hannah's cottage after milking, it was with the sole intention of annoying her. I whined about the heat, the bugs, the rain, and the blisters on my still tender feet. Day after day, we sat together on her front porch while I unfurled my tale of woe. I complained about everything. Then one day, after I'd finished my usual litany, she said, "It must be lonely up there."

The truth in what she said stopped me in my tracks. She was right. It was now more loneliness than wounded vanity that caused my whining. "You can escape the pain of your loneliness," she advised, "if you can find a name for each of your goats."

"I wish you would offer more practical advice," I moaned. "What you're asking is impossible. You're not around them, so you wouldn't know, but a goat is a goat is a goat. They all have floppy ears, they're all brown, and they all say 'Maaaaaaa.' You've seen one goat, you've seen 'em all."

She laid her hand upon my shoulder. "Trust me this once. Do as I ask, and a miracle will happen. Just wait and see."

I didn't put much faith in Hannah's promise of a miracle, but naming them, I thought, would help to pass the time as I moved the herd to and from the barn. I began with the youngest members of the herd. Slowly, a new world opened up to me. I was no longer alone in the pasture. There were Hildy and Martha, who always seemed to forget where they were and wandered near the edge of a gorge. There was James, who would stop grazing to listen to the birds sing. There was Susie, who would nudge and nuzzle me when I sat down for lunch. I lost interest in my complaints and began to entertain Hannah with long and involved stories about my forty-three goats, their relationships, moods, and adventures. I pointed out how their coats glowed, and I bragged about their milk production.

I sit now beneath my favorite tree high in the Summer Hills with Susie by my side. Hannah has promised to bring me lunch today, and I look forward to her arrival. I am trying to write while keeping a careful eye on Rose. She has the sharpest hearing of them all. She'll hear Hannah before I can see her. When Rose lifts her head and turns toward the path, I will know Hannah is coming.

Nighttime ∼

I can't get this afternoon's conversation out of my mind, so I have slipped out of bed to record it by the light of our only candle.

Thanks to Rose, I met Hannah as she topped the rise. She carried a reed basket stocked with sourdough bread, goat cheese (of course), and a bottle of wine. I took the basket from her and gestured toward the tree under which we would picnic. "I'm so glad you're here," I said. "I've been looking forward to this moment all day."

She wiped the sweat that speckled her brow. "So am I, but I think that the path has grown steeper since the last time I climbed it."

A gentle breeze cooled us as we sat under the spreading branches of a white oak tree. Behind us, the Pal-Chin Mountains reached toward the sky, and in the distance in front of us, we could see the ocean meet the horizon. The sky was a sheaf of blue that draped itself across the trees and meadows. I thought of the colors green and blue. Which is more beautiful, earth or sky? We sat in the shade and enjoyed their pageant.

I thanked Hannah again for all she had done. "I really understand how much pain loneliness can cause. When you're in its grip, it drains the life from everything you think and do."

"That's true."

"I've got a surprise for you," I told her. "I've found a remedy for the first of the elders' plagues. It's not that hard when you stop and think about it. If I ever get back home, I'm going to stamp out loneliness."

Hannah leaned back against the tree with an expectant look on her face. I could see she was anxious to hear what I had to say.

"That's right," I gushed, "I'm going to make sure that every elder has some kind of animal, if not his or her own herd of goats."

I had expected Hannah to heap praise upon my insight. Instead, she laughed and laughed and told me that I still had much to learn.

The breeze strengthened, and the leaves over our heads celebrated with their own private music. "You find pleasure in companionship in much the same way you enjoy this shady spot," she said. "It is easy to look up and thank the branches and the leaves for their gifts to us. Likewise, you look at your herd and thank them for soothing the ache of your loneliness."

"Yes," I agreed, "I am thankful to them."

"You are forgetting that the leaves and branches grow from the roots and the soil beneath us. Although we cannot see them, the soil and the roots provide this pool of shade. So it is with companionship. Companionship grows only in the soil of caring relationships. Its roots plunge deep into the heart."

I thought carefully about what she was saying. It seemed to be another case of me pointing to what was tangible and visible, while Hannah went deeper. For her, the truth was to be found among those things that couldn't be seen. "It's not the goats," I said. "It's my relationship with them that's cured my loneliness."

"That's right," Hannah said. "You shouldn't confuse the goats with the gift they have given you. The goats are the same as they always were. It is your relationship to them that has become precious. The elder who cared for the herd before you, died in the storm that brought you here. His relationship to these animals and a long line of their ancestors protected that man from loneliness. The people of the village understood you well enough to give you his work as a gift."

I pulled on my beard and reflected, "Until I knew them, these goats were just four-legged bags of brown fur. My fantasy of providing every elder with an animal misses the point. Without relationships, there can be no companionship."

"Now you are beginning to see how we make life for ourselves here," Hannah replied.

I took a sip of wine and thought this over. I have always enjoyed exploring new ideas, but learning in this way from Hannah was something new for me. She took time to let ideas sink in. She wanted more than the first thought that popped into your head.

Finally, I said, "So, it's really about relationships. . . . Companionship requires proximity."

Hannah agreed but, as usual, phrased the thought in a more elegant way. "Companionship grows in the soil of daily life," she said.

I nodded. "It's like my friends from school. They are still my friends even when they live very far away, but they are no longer my companions."

"The bond you've formed with your goats has healed an empty place inside your heart. That is good."

"It feels good." I thought about the first plague of the elders again and sighed. "Hannah, I don't know how to tell you this, or even if I should, but many of the elderly in the Other World live without the balm of companionship. They have no village on which to rely. Their children and grandchildren live far away. Some live in houses where there is no love."

I got up and started pacing around the base of the tree. I wasn't talking to Hannah so much as thinking out loud. "The frailest of our elders are sometimes sent into institutions where they are surrounded by doctors and nurses who actually believe they should not love the elders. They believe they can "fix" old people by giving them medicines and treatments of all descriptions. They know them only through their diseases. These elderly have been condemned to a life among strangers." As I finished speaking, I suddenly felt sick at the thought of the suffering they endure.

Hannah was silent for several minutes. Finally, she spoke slowly, "I remember people in the Other World saying, 'Love is blind.' How wrong they were. Love opens our eyes. It shows us things we cannot see if we are strangers. It takes us places strangers cannot go."

There was nothing I could say. I looked out over the herd. Hildy and Martha were at it again. They had wandered near the edge of the gorge. I hurriedly excused myself and trotted across the meadow to retrieve them. When I returned, Hannah looked at me sadly.

"The elders of the Other World are carrying a heavy burden," she said. "To love and to feel loved can heal many ills. You know this. You have felt this magic in your own life. I do not believe that you will ever return to the Other World. However, if you do, you must promise me that you will do your best to see that the elders are given all of the love they need."

She looked away from me and, speaking so softly that I had to strain to catch the words, said, "Elders draw strength from a village just as a babe draws strength from its mother's breast. How could a mother turn away from her babe when he cries from hunger? Pity the child born to such a woman. How could a village turn away from its elders when they wither from loneliness? Pity the elders of the Other World."

Without another word, she gathered her things and left. I watched her as she disappeared down the footpath. Then I returned to my goats. I wandered among them and examined the pasture. It was time to move them to higher ground. I whistled sharply and called to them. They knew what I wanted, and soon we were on our way.

Having all of this on paper, I can now see what Hannah was trying to teach me:

> Loving companionship is the antidote to loneliness. In a human community, we must provide easy access to human and animal companionship.

Haleigh's Apprentice

Last quarter of the full moon ～

$\mathcal{J}$ WAS SO PREOCCUPIED during my first few weeks as a goatherd that I barely noticed how Jude was doing as a gardener. At the end of each day, we both fell into bed, exhausted from our unaccustomed exertions. She told me little other than that Haleigh was not easy to please and the work was hard. It wasn't until I began naming my goats that I noticed Jude was beginning to sing softly to herself in the evenings as I wrote in my journal. Clearly, something had changed. Still, the only thing she would say when I asked her about her work was that Haleigh's lessons were like Hannah's, only louder.

"Let me use your journal, Bill," she said this evening. "I want to explain—to myself more than anyone else—what I've learned from Haleigh."

Unlike Bill, I was pleased with Hannah's decision. After our long convalescence, I wanted to do something useful, and the village had no use for an academic gerontologist. I liked the idea of working in the garden. My mom's green thumb had always appealed to me, from a distance. Gardening seemed a charming pastime, at least for her. I was too busy. Every time Mom invited me to join her in the garden, I put her off with excuses. Eventually, she stopped asking. I've always felt guilty about that. This would give me a chance to redeem myself.

I also thought I saw a hidden message in Hannah's comments. She had to know that I was, at best, a novice gardener. Surely, my true occupation would be looking after Haleigh. Bill and I had done the math earlier. If Hannah had come to Kallimos about eighty years ago and Haleigh was already a young woman then, that would put Haleigh at or near the century mark. A woman of her years would need someone to take care of her. I felt honored that Hannah asked me.

My heart was singing with what I now recognize was an unhealthy mixture of pride and compassion when I walked into the garden that first morning. I saw an old woman kneeling alongside a patch of vegetables. As there was no one else in sight, I walked up and knelt down beside her. Speaking slowly and distinctly, I introduced myself. She looked at me as if I were some kind of bug.

"Give me your hands, girl," she ordered.

I thought she wanted to hold hands, so I reached out to take hers into mine. She grabbed my hands and turned them palm up. "Worse than I thought," she muttered, rolling her eyes as she stood up.

"Is something wrong?" I asked in my most endearing voice.

"It's a mystery of the universe how you ever got yourself a bellyful of food with hands like those," she huffed.

Befuddled, I looked closely at my hands. "What's wrong with them?"

Haleigh shook her head in disgust. "They're soft, girl, and more than likely the rest of you is soft, too."

This woman would take some getting used to, I decided. I'd never met a person so old and still so full of vinegar. Hannah speaks softly and has manners to match. Haleigh hollers. Subtlety is unknown to her.

Within five minutes of our initial meeting, Haleigh had marched me to the bean patch and set me to work weeding. While she toted basket after basket of peas to her front porch, I wilted under the glow of the mid-morning sun. Tiny bugs with a nasty bite swarmed around my face and arms. My back throbbed. I was thirsty and tired.

The sun was high in the sky, and I was still on my hands and knees when she came back to check on me. I had stuck it out. I hadn't complained, and I'd accomplished more than a little. Unfortunately, I had also pulled up half the bean crop along with the weeds. Haleigh exploded when she saw the devastation I had wrecked. She spit curses and hurled insults. She stamped her feet and wailed. All I could do was cry.

As suddenly as it had started, her tantrum stopped. She looked down at me, at the piles of withered bean seedlings, at me again, and then she laughed. Somewhere in this disaster, she had found some kind of absurd humor. Her laughter was as full-bodied and rich as her fury. The guffaw seemed to rise from her toes. Her body rocked with gales of laughter, and tears came to her eyes. Struggling to contain herself, the old woman I had imagined myself taking care of pulled me to my feet, put her arm around my shoulders, and tousled my hair. She led me to her cottage and, recognizing how tired I was, made a place for me to lie down. While I slept, she sat on the front porch and shelled four baskets of peas.

When I awoke from my nap, she told me that she was sorry for what had happened. "You are the most peculiar person I have ever met," she said. "When I look at you, I see the body of a grown woman. But in truth, you are still a child."

Her words offended me. "That's not true," I protested.

"Yes, it is, child. You have baby's hands. You confuse the weeds and the fruits. You know none of the songs, the chants, the traditions of the garden." She smiled and touched my face with her calloused fingers. "Tomorrow will be a new day. You have a good heart. You deserve another beginning."

She busied herself making tea and then invited me to sit on the porch with her. We talked as we drank our tea, and then she sent me home.

So ended my first day in Haleigh's garden.

In spite of that bewildering start, or maybe because of it, we have made peace with each other. Clearly, I am the student, and she is the master. Though I hate to admit it, there was a lot of truth in what she claimed that first day. I was a child. I had dismissed as nothing more than nonstop arts and crafts the thousands of tasks and duties that go into making a life here. I had enjoyed the peacefulness of this life but had thought it was the result of simple, thoughtless labor. When you watch the tasks being done from the shady comfort of your front porch, they look easy enough. You only discover how difficult they are when you set your hands to them. The work here is hard, and more and more each day, so am I.

Every day, Haleigh and I aim for an early start. The work varies but the routine is constant, because it's no fun to get behind and have to be out in the midday sun. Haleigh, of course, oversees the entire garden, but together we tend its largest section. That is something to be proud of because space is apportioned according to skill. Most of our time is spent weeding, watering, mulching, tilling, and fertilizing.

Haleigh insists that neither plants nor people should be fooled with during the heat of the day. When the sun climbs high in the sky, we retreat to her porch. We talk and sing as we shell peas, snap beans, and peel potatoes, eluding the afternoon sun. Haleigh has taught me many of the stories and songs of Kallimos. I am proud to say that I am now more fluent in the language than Bill. That's because I am with Haleigh all day long and he is with his goats. HA!

At first, I was shy about chanting along with Haleigh in the garden. It seemed silly to think that chanting would help a garden. It seemed even sillier to think that one song should be sung while weeding but not while harvesting, and another should be sung while watering but only when the moon is in its waning phase. When Haleigh told me that these rules exist because the songs are magic and must be used with great care, it was my turn to laugh. Now that I've seen with my own eyes her fantastic ability to cultivate the earth, I have become a believer. There may be no supporting research to back it up, but with results like hers, who cares?

Haleigh has shown me that caring means helping things to grow. She nurtures everything she touches. I can feel it when we are together. We've been together for only two moons, and already she knows me better than anybody but Bill. I don't know how she does it, but somehow she looks into my heart and understands what she sees there. And I am not alone. No wonder Haleigh was chosen to raise Hannah.

The Three Sisters

The half moon ～

THIS IS MY FIRST CHANCE to get back to my journal since Jude's entry. The heat has been unbearable the past few days. The sky is painfully blue, and the leaves hang limp on the trees. I have decided to keep the goats in the barn, where I can be sure that they will get enough forage and water; the pastures are too dry to risk grazing. Jude is worried about the garden. Haleigh says that as long as the heat wave continues they will have to carry water to the garden from the river. I'm afraid going back and forth between the river and the garden will be exhausting for both of them.

Evening ～

Once I got the goats fed and watered this morning, I joined Haleigh and Jude in their work. Haleigh had put out a call for help with the watering. It was damn hard work. The sun bore down on us, and I could see that it was taking its toll on Haleigh, as I had feared it would. She walked unsteadily, and sweat ran from her brow. I pointed this out to Jude.

"We've got to do something for Haleigh," I said. "She shouldn't be out in this heat."

"She'll do what she thinks is best," Jude answered.

"She's baking like a potato," I protested.

"Haleigh doesn't take kindly to being told what's good for her. If you know what's good for you, you'll let her be. Let's get back to work."

I did so but kept my eye on Haleigh; the hotter it got, the further she drooped. Everyone else saw this just as clearly as I did, but no one seemed to care, which made me very angry. As I saw it, it was my duty as a physician to take action.

I walked up to her and said, "Give me those buckets. You really shouldn't be doing all this heavy work in this heat."

Haleigh set the pail on the ground and answered me curtly, "I'll be all right."

"No, you won't. You're on the edge of heat stroke, and you better get into the shade and rest or you're likely to collapse." I snatched the buckets away before she could pick them up. "Haleigh, we've got plenty of help. The job is nearly done. I want you to sit down and get something to drink."

She glared at me from under the brim of her straw hat. Her voice descended into a growl, "Trying to push me out of the garden, are you? Want to set me aside like an old shoe, do you?"

The other villagers backed quickly away from where we were standing. Even Jude cleared out. "It's not that at all," I said soothingly. "I just want you to be safe. Working out here isn't healthy for you. I have every reason to be concerned about you."

She spat on the ground. "That's what I think of your concern," she said. "I was here tending this garden before your grandparents were born. This is my garden. My hands make it grow, and when the time comes I'll be buried here, and then my body will make it grow." She moved a step closer to me, and I stepped back. "You might as well bury me alive as ask me to leave it when it needs me."

"You've got it all wrong," I tried to explain. "I'm not saying anything like that. It's just that we have plenty of help and I think you could use some rest."

Her voice rose with her temper. "You are a crazy, hard-hearted fool. I'll leave this garden when the breath of life leaves my body. Is that what you want? Are you trying to kill me?"

The force of her outburst left her quivering with rage. Without another word, I held the buckets out to her. She took them and, sputtering and grumbling, trudged away from me.

As soon as it seemed safe, Jude returned to my side. She spoke to me in the soft, mocking, singsong voice that every child knows. "I told you so, I told you so."

"I was concerned, and I acted out of kindness," I replied defensively.

"You threatened her, and she let you have it."

I glowered. "I didn't threaten her. How can you call anything I said a threat? That's ridiculous."

"No, it isn't."

"It was simple kindness."

"It's simple kindness in the Other World. Here, people know better," Jude said as we walked toward a plot of pale green cornstalks. She went on, "I learned my lesson about a month ago. It was hot that day, too, and Haleigh and I had to hill and mulch the potatoes. It was heavy work, and I watched her closely. By mid-morning she was leaning heavily on her hoe."

We poured our water onto the scorched plants and turned once again toward the river. "Like you," Jude continued, "I told her to go back to the porch and let me finish. I told her I was worried about her and that if she lived in the Other World she wouldn't have to work in the hot sun at this time in her life. She could rest all day. Kallimos has no word for retirement, so I had to explain the whole 'golden-years, retirement-living, no-work, all-play' concept to her. She told me I was a fool if I believed any such thing."

"What happened?"

"I backed off, and when the work was done, she told me a story. After the scene you made today, I wouldn't be surprised if we hear that story again sometime soon."

"So you're saying I'm in for a lecture?"

"It's not a lecture."

"Well, she can tell all the stories she wants, but I was right and she was wrong."

Jude refused to rise to the bait, so we worked the remainder of the morning in silence.

That afternoon, the dozen or so of us who had been watering the garden gathered on Haleigh's front porch. We replenished ourselves with gallons of a cool, mint-flavored water that left the mouth cool even after the mug was empty. After a period of joshing and laughter, we grew quiet. Then one of the men spoke up, "Tell us a story, Haleigh."

She responded, "A story? On a day like this? No, no, it is too hot for a story."

A woman piped up, "Please, Haleigh, tell us a story. We've worked so hard; take us away to the ancient days."

The children chimed in excitedly. "Give us a story. You must tell us one! We've worked so hard, and we've saved the garden!"

Haleigh began to relent. "Well, perhaps it wouldn't hurt." This allowance spurred her audience on, and at last, she agreed to tell a tale. But what story should be told? Another wave of good-natured banter followed. Over the rim of my mug, I watched the whole process the way I used to watch children playing in a sandbox. I found it quite enjoyable. Finally, a familiar voice rang out from behind me. It was Jude.

"I want to hear the tale of the three sisters."

All the other voices fell quiet. I knew at once that I was the only one present who did not know the story. It was also clear that it dealt in some way with my confrontation with Haleigh. I breathed a heavy sigh. My comeuppance was apparently at hand.

Haleigh rocked gently back and forth in the woven chair that hung from the porch ceiling. She took a sip from the brown mug she cradled in her hands and began her story.

Listen well, my children, for I am about to tell you of a time long, long ago. I will tell of the day the Earth was born. Her older sisters, the Moon and the Sun, glowed with joyous anticipation. The Moon was the elder of the sisters, and like the hair of the Elders of the People, she shone with the dazzling brilliance of silver. The Sun shone as brightly as her sister, but her rays gleamed with the golden glow of youth. They talked excitedly of their hopes for their sister, who would surely outshine them both. Oh, the glory of it all! The Three Sisters would illuminate the farthest corners of the heavens with their unquenchable fire.

Sadly, it was not to be. The Earth was born dark and cold. She could not see, nor could she speak. The Sun and the Moon gave themselves over to their grief, and for many ages, they wept for their newborn sister. Their tears filled the seas, the lakes, and the rivers. Even to this day, the Sun mourns the Earth's grim fate. The tears she sheds make the rain that falls upon our heads.

The sisters feared the Earth would be frightened in the darkness that surrounded her, so they resolved to shine upon her and keep her warm for all time. For many ages, the Earth found mute comfort in her sisters' loving gaze. During the day, the Sun cast a gentle glow upon her face. At night, the Moon shone upon her with equal brilliance. Together, they held the darkness at bay.

In time, the Sun began to worry about the Moon. It was clear to see that her rays no longer cast the golden light of youth. The Sun wondered if the strain of caring for their sister would overcome her. The thought made her tremble in fear. If the Moon left her, she would be alone in the sky forever.

Perhaps, she thought, the Moon would benefit from a rest. She told her sister of her concerns. The Moon said, "I am honored by your concern, dear Sister, but do not fear. My light is silver, yours is gold, but the love I feel for our dear sister gives me strength. I am well." Those brave words failed to reassure the Sun, and her anxiety grew with the passing of the ages. Repeatedly, she pointed out her sister's frailties and beseeched her to rest. Finally, the Moon relented and honored her sister's wishes. The Moon quenched her fires, and darkness fell for the first time upon the face of the Earth. Keeping her promise to the Moon, the Sun shone with a doubled brilliance. For the first time, her rays burned her little sister's face. This is how the great desert on the far side of the mountains came to be.

While the Moon rested, the Sun grew weary. Shining so brightly was more difficult than she had imagined, and she was lonely. She missed her older sister's satin words of wisdom and encouragement. Still, she endured. She was proud of the vigor that let her do the work of two.

Finally, the time came to wake the Moon from her slumber. The Sun called to her once, but she did not answer. The Sun raised her voice and called again. The Moon remained silent. The Sun called a third time, this time with all her might. Her voice shook the cosmos, and its force shattered her rays into little pieces. These specks of light fled in terror from her mighty voice and did not stop until they had reached the farthest corners of the heavens. This is how the stars came to be.

At last, the Moon responded. Her voice rattled and cracked. The Sun had to strain to catch the words. "Let me rest, sister, let me rest. I am old, I am tired, and I will shine no more." Despite the Sun's desperate pleas, the Moon fell silent and was never heard from again. Shame for what she had done filled the Sun. This is why sunrises and sunsets are crimson. The Sun is recalling her great shame.

Now, the Sun is alone. During the day, she pours her light and heat down upon her little sister, the Earth. At night, she shines upon her older sister, the Moon, as she tosses and turns in her sleep. That is why the moon waxes and wanes in the night sky.

The burden the Sun carries is heavy. She carries it alone, and she will carry it forever. Still, even the mighty must sometimes rest. For this reason, the winter is cooler than the summer.

That's the way it was and that's the way it is.

Hunger finally stirred us from our places, and we left Haleigh's porch. I decided to stop at the barn to check the goats' water, so Jude headed home alone. When she got there, she found Zachary sitting cross-legged on our front porch. Draped across his lap was a two-foot-long fish that must have weighed half as much as he did.

"I caught this for you," he told Jude.

"How did you ever catch such a big fish?" she asked.

"It's easy. I go to the shore when the big waves come. The big fish always come when the big waves come. The bigger the waves, the bigger the fish."

"Thank you for the fish, Zachary, but I'm afraid I don't know how to prepare it," Jude said.

"That's all right, I'll help you."

He showed Jude how to clean the fish and, after swearing her to secrecy, revealed the secret fishing spot where he catches the "big ones." She couldn't understand him completely, but it seems that he goes out at low tide, wades out to a boulder that lies just off shore, and then waits for the fish. When he's patient, he doesn't even need to swim. Jude told him to be careful and gave him a kiss. With that, he was out the door and on to new adventures.

The full moon ⁓

I'm staying at the barn tonight. My favorite doe, Rose, is not well, and I need to be with her. Jude promised me she would join me in my vigil for the first half of the night. Looking out the window, I watched her as she approached the barn, accompanied only by her silent shadow. I met her at the door and took her into my arms. I held her close to me and then kissed her softly on the lips and told her I loved her. I stepped back and

admired the moonlit figure of the woman who is my mate for life. Then we sat side by side on the floor of the barn and talked.

We reminisced about our old lives and the day we met. We spoke of those we had left behind. We voiced the doubts we now share about The Book. We struggled to understand how something that had seemed so bright, smart, and true could now seem so terribly wrong. Finally, the conversation turned toward the three sisters.

"That really was a cute story Haleigh told." I said.

"It wasn't cute," Jude responded. "She was trying to teach you something."

"Maybe," I said, "but I think she was really just covering for her own insecurities. Haleigh may not like to admit it, but she is a very old woman and she needs help. If you ask me, she should learn how to ask for help and receive it gracefully."

"You're the one who needs to accept help gracefully."

"What are you talking about?"

"She told the story for you. She was taking care of you."

"I saw what she was doing, but it doesn't change the fact that she needs help, and she's got to learn how to accept it without making a scene."

Jude sat up straight and looked me in the eye. "You still don't get it, do you?" she said a little angrily. "She did ask for help, and she did receive it gracefully. She asked for an assistant, and the village gave her me. Then she knew we needed help getting the garden watered and was glad to have everyone there. Everyone else was willing to let her decide what she needed. You were the only one who thought you knew better than she did."

"Maybe, but how are they going to feel when she keels over in the garden someday?" I asked.

"I think they'll be happy."

"Then they don't really care about her."

"No, not happy that she's gone, happy that she lived her life the way she wanted."

"I think it's elder abuse," I said stubbornly. "She's old. She shouldn't have to work at all."

Jude bit her lip in frustration and then, "Remember the second plague that Hannah told us about? She said that helplessness preys upon the elders and that it is the duty of the village to protect them from it. Haleigh has shown me that balancing the giving and the receiving of care is the best protection there is against helplessness. When I wanted to hill the potatoes myself, Haleigh said, 'Whenever you see an elder who gives nothing to the village but receives everything from the village, know that death stands beside that bed.'

"So open your eyes, Bill. At home, we force the elderly to trade their independence for the help they need. Getting support means living with less freedom. That makes them fearful of asking for assistance. Here, Haleigh can ask for help and keep her independence."

I thought about what Jude said. As a physician, I was accustomed to people seeking my advice and accepting my authority. Haleigh had asked for my help, and I had gladly given it to her. The problem was that I had wanted to give too much, and she had rebuked me loudly and publicly. I had thought I was the only person who cared about her well-being. Now I saw that I was alone in expecting her to surrender her freedom.

Perhaps the best way to explain Haleigh's lesson is this:

> To give care to another makes us stronger. To receive care gracefully is a pleasure and an art. A healthy human community promotes both of these virtues in its daily life, seeking always to balance one with the other.

Turtle Eggs

J WOULD LIKE TO BE MORE DILIGENT in my journal keeping. The rains came just days after my last entry, and the heat of high summer has relented. A moon has passed, and I have been very busy. The goats and I have returned to the Summer Hills, and they are feasting on the rejuvenated pastures. Rose is once again in good health. Jude tells me that the garden has come through the dry weather nicely and that she and Haleigh are anticipating a fine harvest.

We experienced an unexpected pleasure a few days back. Usually, we are in bed soon after the sun "goes to the moon," as the people here say. For the first time since our arrival in Kallimos, however, the day was followed by a long, strange, exhilarating night.

It began in the usual way. The morning was cool with a gentle, northerly breeze. By midday, the breeze was gone and the sun was beating down, though with the approach of autumn the heat was less intense. Jude and I worked all day, and when we returned home in the late afternoon, our tunics were caked with the salt of dried sweat. We ate a light meal, sat on the porch, and visited with the neighbors. Zachary and I played Tee-Ho-Nan, a village game that requires a stick and a ball and, like baseball, has rules that are hard to explain. Unlike the games I grew up with, there are no winners or losers. The players cooperate to keep the ball inside the marked boundaries for as long as possible. After the game, we sat on the porch and talked. We fell gratefully into bed.

We were sleeping peacefully when the sound of the front door being thrown open woke us. In the dim moonlight I could see Zachary in the doorway. He ran right up to our bed and leaned over its edge. Pulling at my arm, he cried, "They're here, they're here, they're here! Come on, get up! Let's go! They're here!"

I pulled myself up onto my elbows and grumbled back, "Who's here?"

His eyes grew wide. "The turtle eggs . . . right now, on the beach. We have to go!" And with that, he raced out the door even faster than he had entered.

By this time, a commotion outside our door had replaced the usual late evening calm. Jude and I clambered out of bed and pulled on our clothes. As we stepped onto the front porch, we saw Hannah scurrying toward us with a stack of wicker baskets in her arms. We expected her to stop and tell us what was happening. Instead, she tossed us two of the baskets and kept going. "Come on, get going, they're here. The turtle eggs are here!" she called back to us as she disappeared down the path that led to the beach. Her step was so light and her heart so merry that I think she could have outraced Zachary.

As we looked out across the village green, we could see that everyone in the village was headed toward the beach. Excitement and joy filled the air. We grabbed the baskets Hannah had tossed, and we fell in with those who were bringing up the rear of the procession. What else could we do? We made our way down the path and soon caught up with Haleigh. Happily, she was willing to explain this insanity to us.

"For longer than anyone can remember, the turtles have come to our beach to lay their eggs. They come just once a year, and we never know when they will arrive. They bury their eggs in the sand, and we have only one night to find them. If we miss that night, the eggs turn bitter and cannot be eaten."

"All this fuss is over turtle eggs?" I asked. But before I would receive an answer, an unpleasant conclusion dawned on me. Suddenly, I felt a little woozy. Those delicious pickled eggs I enjoyed so much came from turtles?

The footpath descended gradually, winding its way between the trees and opening abruptly onto the beach. I was unprepared for what greeted me there. The moonlight glittered on the sea like thousands of restless, fallen stars, and the sand had a blood-red glow from dozens of blazing torches. Men, women, and children, all on their hands and knees, huddled inside the torches' shimmering pools of light. With their bare hands, they were carefully opening freshly turned mounds of sand.

Zachary raced up to us. He took our hands and led us to one of the mounds. As he skipped off to check in with his father, Jude and I knelt down in the still warm sand. Within minutes, we had unearthed a clutch of turtle eggs. We had just transferred them from the nest to our basket when we heard Haleigh behind us. Her voice was filled with alarm. "What," she cried out, "are you doing?"

"We're harvesting the eggs," I answered confidently.

She put her hands on her hips and looked like she was about to explode, but she hesitated for a moment. Then she erupted in laughter. "It is a wonder how you two ever survived before you came here," she declared.

"Only a fool would take all the eggs from a nest. The wise take only one egg from each nest, and always choose the smallest of those they find. The stories say that the turtles have been coming since long before our ancestors became part of this world. Over those long ages, we have come to depend on these eggs as a part of our diet. If we took all of the eggs, or even the best of them, the turtles would stop coming to our shore."

Zachary had returned in time to hear the end of Haleigh's explanation. He chimed in, "The turtles trust us. That's why they come back every year. On the night of the turtle eggs, we get to stay up all night and dig up all of the nests on this beach. It's the happiest night of all." Already I could hear the sounds of drumming and singing rising from the people at the other end of the beach. "Don't worry, by morning all our baskets will be full."

Jude and I looked guiltily at our basket and the empty nest in front of us. Without a word, we started putting the eggs back into the nest.

We spent the rest of the night with Zachary and Haleigh, shoulder to shoulder, digging in the sand. Music filled the air, and shooting stars ran across the clear night sky. The gray light that comes before the dawn had just broken over the mountains when we returned to the village and our beds. The air was still and the quiet very deep. It seemed as though the village itself slept. The rest was well deserved.

Three days have passed since the night of the turtle eggs, and the excitement is just beginning to subside. The first night, everyone was tired and went to bed early. On the second day, we celebrated with a feast that began at noon and ran well into the evening. Now another day has passed, and tonight the village is quiet. You can almost feel the spell wearing off. My mind, however, keeps revisiting yesterday's feast. It was a turning point for me. For the first time, I publicly and without reservation, accepted Kallimos as my home.

The sun had just set when Jude and I came upon Haleigh and Hannah sitting near the green's central fire pit. When they saw us, their conversation came to an abrupt halt. It was obvious they had been talking about us.

We sat down beside them and exchanged pleasant observations on the coolness of the evening and the swiftness with which the day had passed. After a moment or two, Haleigh spoke her mind. "Hannah and I," she said, "are proud of you two. More proud than we ever thought we'd be." A smile lit her face as she spoke.

This was high praise indeed, and we basked in its glow for about five seconds. Then we wondered what she meant by "more proud than we ever thought we'd be." Sure, we were injured and exhausted when we first arrived on Kallimos, but other than that, why wouldn't she be proud of us? Hannah sensed our mixed emotions.

"I don't think you understand how pitiable we found you to be when you arrived here," she said.

"You're right about that," I laughed. "We were pretty battered and bruised."

"I'll bet we were the talk of the village," Jude added.

Hannah said, "No, that's not what I mean. Your appearance was easy enough to accept." She shifted her weight as though she was sitting on an uncomfortable rock. "Until we met you, we did not know that people could live with so little faith in their hearts—so little faith in themselves, in others, in the world that surrounds them, in life itself. It was easy to see that you trusted no one and nothing, not even yourselves."

Although we didn't like them, her words rang true. We had not trusted Hannah when she first cared for us. We had not trusted the way of life that was stretched out before us when we watched the village from our porch. Finally, I said, "When we lived there in the Other World, we were smart, important people. We believed we didn't have to trust anything or anyone. We thought faith was for weaklings."

"Faith is strong, people are weak," Haleigh clucked.

"I was taught that if you can control something, you don't need trust," Jude said. "The more things you can control, the less you have to trust. People who can build their lives completely around things they can control, don't need faith at all."

Hannah said, "But that kind of life isn't worth living. Faith—or trust that life or the world that surrounds us has meaning—is what gives us the strength to be human beings. With it, we can endure and overcome suffering. Without it, our afflictions crush us. With it, we can savor unexpected pleasures. Without it, fear is our constant companion."

I looked at Jude. "She's right, you know. If we had washed up on a shore far from the village, we would have died of anger and fear, not hunger and thirst." I took a deep breath. "The fact is that I'm ready to accept my place here," I said. "This is the life I have been given to lead, and I am going to live it."

Tears welled in Jude's eyes. I suddenly realized that she had gotten to this point ahead of me and had trusted that I would join her. Her trust had been rewarded, and now she was happy. We had declared Kallimos our home, but it had accepted us long before we had accepted it.

The people here have an uncanny sense of the moment. Just as I cast my lot with Kallimos, a line of singers and dancers approached. Zachary and his father were leading them, and they signaled us to join them. Many hands reached out to pull us to our feet.

The lives Jude and I lead here are as heavily spiced as the food we eat. The rigid, controlled existence we knew is slipping away, and we are glad to let it go. We have acquired a taste for this kind of living. We are no longer too embarrassed to join in the celebrations the people of Kallimos make for themselves. In the Other World, I listened to recordings of professional musicians and felt ashamed at my lack of talent. Here, I bang drums and blow pipes along with everyone else.

It is not just the traditions, rituals, and holidays that we enjoy. Underneath these major events flows an ever-present current of spontaneity and laughter. In New York City, we were entertained by some of the finest performers on the planet. Here, we laugh, play, and celebrate with people we know and love.

The work of digging up hundreds of turtle nests on short notice could have been imposed on the young or the old of Kallimos, but it wasn't. It could seem like a burden, but it didn't. Instead, the night and the days that followed were infused with the spirit of life, love, and laughter. Jude and I dug turtle nests with an old woman and a young boy, and we were glad for their company.

Trust in each other allows us the pleasure of answering the needs of the moment. When we fill our lives with variety and spontaneity, we honor the world and our place in it.

Caleb's Basket

The full moon ∿

THE GOATS ARE DRY. Bill has taken the herd high into the Summer Hills where they can savor the fresh pastures and go about the business of breeding. They have given us milk through the spring and summer, but now this is their time. They will spend the winter in the barn, give birth in the spring, and again treat us to their milk. So it goes, round and round.

I miss Bill, and somehow writing the day's events in his journal makes him seem closer. Haleigh knows how much I miss him and has, in her usual irascible way, found ways for us to spend more time together. I sit on her porch in the evening, and we talk. Mostly, we talk about little things. She is full to bursting with stories, and the slightest thing can bring a story to her lips. If she sees a woman walk by with an armful of flowers, she'll say, "You know, it's the strangest thing about those flowers." Then she'll launch into a long, involved story about the flowers. She'll tell me how they came to have their current shape, color, and scent and then teach me their uses. At first, I accepted her tales as simple fables, but I have now come to see them as much more than that. There is always a story within the story, a lesson hidden inside the lesson.

This morning while we worked in the garden, I prattled on about all the important things we had learned—the power of trust, the three plagues of the elderly, and all the rest. Haleigh listened carefully to everything I had to say and asked me a long series of questions that I did my best to answer. I could see she had something on her mind, so I wasn't surprised when, after our noon meal, she called to the children playing on the green instead of taking her customary siesta. When they heard her voice, they came running, their eyes open wide with excitement.

The children here continue to amaze me. They are so different from the children I knew in the Other World. It is hard to imagine those children responding with such joy to the call of an old woman. In that world, now that I think of it, old women and young children spend very little time together. It is as if they live in separate, parallel worlds. Here, Haleigh knows all of the children's names and all of their parents and grandparents.

Something else separates these children from the ones I knew before we came to Kallimos. They are comfortable with each other and with their place in the village. I don't see the teasing and bullying I remember from childhood. Watching them makes me want to be a child again. There are days when I wish I had been born here.

Anyway, the children tumbled onto the porch, and Haleigh beamed at them as they formed a semicircle around her. As usual, Zachary found his way to my lap and snuggled right in. I remember the first time I saw Haleigh call the children to her for a story. I stood off to the side, feeling like an intruder. She noticed that I was missing from the circle and searched for me with her eyes. When she found me, she signaled for me to sit down. Of course, I complied. Even so, I felt uncomfortable and out of place. Haleigh sensed my discomfort and winked at me, which made me feel better. Now, I feel completely at home.

Given Haleigh's reaction to our earlier conversation, I had no doubt that today's story would have something to do with the ideas I had been discussing that morning. I have begun to appreciate how people teach and learn here. There are no professors, no organized courses of study. Instead, an event, a dispute, a crisis, or a celebration serves as a signal for one of the elders to teach a lesson by telling a story or singing a song.

Haleigh closed her eyes, sat back in her chair, and waited for the children to settle in. When they were quiet, she began the story, the way she always does, in the fashion of Kallimos.

❖ ❖ ❖

A long time ago, when The People were still new to this world, there was an Elder whom it is our duty to remember. His name was Caleb, and he lived alone in the forest far away from the Village.

The children gasped at that, at the strange courage of this elder. "Haleigh!" they said, "Caleb lived alone? He had no home in the Village? How did he live? What did he eat? Where did he sleep?" Haleigh held up her hands at all the questions and then went on.

Caleb's home was the forest. His companions were the trees, the streams, and the wild creatures of the woods. The forest understood and nourished Caleb just as the Village understands and nourishes you. The People said that Caleb was the wisest of all Elders, and they sought his counsel when they wished to have an answer to a difficult question. But while many sought Caleb, few found him, for he spent his days wandering through the hills and valleys of the forest. These he moved through with the silent beauty of a star twinkling in the night sky. Only those who persevered in their search gained the pleasure of his company. It is said he leant his ear and shared his wisdom the way the Sun gives us warmth and light.

Now there happened to be a young man in the Village who wanted, more than anything else, to be wise beyond his years. His name was Samuel. When Samuel heard all of The People's stories about Caleb, he resolved to leave the Village and find this wonderful, wise man. While others sought Caleb to find the solution to a problem, Samuel wished to become Caleb's student. He wanted to walk side by side with Caleb. He wanted to learn his secrets, his truths, and his wisdom.

On the day he became a man, Samuel went to his parents. He told them of his desire to leave the Village and search for Caleb. With his pack already filled with provisions, he kissed his mother and father good-bye, and set out on his quest.

After several lonely and frustrating weeks of searching, Samuel came upon Caleb as the Elder sat on the bank of a small stream. It was just as the Village Elders had said. Caleb welcomed him warmly. They shared a simple meal, and Samuel poured out his heart to the wise old man. He told him about his life in the Village and his burning desire to find wisdom. "Caleb," he asked, "will you be my teacher?"

Caleb considered Samuel's request while he watched light and shadow chase each other across the surface of the stream. The gentle rays of the late afternoon sun cut through the canopy overhead. Finally, he turned to the young man and said, "Yes, young Samuel, you may join me."

The old man rose from his resting place, but before Samuel could gather his pack, the Elder had disappeared down a dark and twisting forest path. This sudden departure surprised Samuel. His provisions lay in a heap on the stream bank. If he took time to repack them, he would lose Caleb's trail. Samuel took one last look at his belongings, shrugged his shoulders, and started down the path in pursuit of Caleb.

Many seasons passed. The two men visited every corner of the forest. Samuel came to know the forest's hills, valleys, and streams nearly as well as Caleb knew them. The master and his student spent many days in silent contemplation. They would often lose themselves in the play of sunlight on the face of a hillside or in the reflections cast by a limpid pool of water. Days and sometimes weeks would go by without a single word passing from Caleb's lips. Only on the rarest of occasions would Caleb actually instruct his student. Samuel loved these long, thoughtful conversations. They whetted his appetite for knowledge and wisdom.

As the seasons passed, Samuel became convinced that he deserved much more. His patience wore thin. The young man began muttering under his breath. He recited his grievances as he tramped through the forest. "Why won't Caleb teach me every day? What is he waiting for? Doesn't he trust me? Why am I wasting my time with this old man?"

One day, when they had stopped by the shore of a lake deep in the forest, Samuel's frustration bubbled over. He confronted Caleb, saying, "Caleb, I left my home and my family to be your student. I have traveled with you and been your faithful companion for many seasons because I seek your wisdom and your knowledge. I have been gentle and patient, but now my heart is full of anger. I have done much for you and I have given much to you, but you offer me your wisdom only on the rarest occasions." The veins in his neck bulged as he spoke.

When the young man's anger was spent, Caleb put his arm around Samuel's shoulder and walked with him to the edge of the lake. Standing side by side, they looked out at the water. At last, Caleb spoke. "When the morning light comes again, I will make everything clear to you. Tomorrow will be our last day together. You are ready to return to the Village with all that you have learned."

Samuel watched the stars walk across the sky that night. A combination of fear and excitement stirred his soul. His fear was that his outburst had offended his gentle teacher. His excitement came from Caleb's promise to teach him what he needed to know. He fell asleep as dawn broke.

Not surprisingly, Caleb was the first one up. He busied himself preparing for Samuel's last lesson. By the time his young student awoke, all was ready. Caleb called him down to the edge of the lake.

"Samuel, look at my basket closely. Can you tell me if it is full?" The question puzzled Samuel, but he did as he was told. He picked up the basket and looked into its depth. It seemed ordinary enough. It was empty.

"Master, you know as well as I that this basket is empty," Samuel replied, returning the basket to Caleb.

Caleb then took a half dozen coconut-sized stones and placed them carefully in the basket. When he was done, he asked again, "Is my basket full?"

The question again puzzled Samuel. "Yes, of course, it is full now. I watched you fill it with those stones."

"No, Samuel, my basket is not full." Caleb reached down and picked up a handful of pebbles. He poured several measures of pebbles into the basket. At last, they filled the spaces between the stones. "I ask you again," Caleb said. "Is my basket full?"

Samuel frowned for a moment and then answered, "Now, Master, it's obvious that the basket is full."

"No, Samuel, my basket is not full." This time the old man took a handful of sand and poured it into the basket. He added handful after handful until the sand filled all of the spaces between the pebbles. Samuel looked on in disbelief. "I ask you again," said Caleb. "Is my basket full?"

A smile broke over Samuel's face, and he roared his answer. "Yes, now the basket is full!"

The teacher shook his head. "No, my basket is not full." Caleb produced the skin in which he carried his drinking water. He poured its contents into the basket, and the water filled the spaces between the grains of sand. Then Caleb said, "Now, my basket is full."

Caleb continued, "Samuel, you have been my companion and friend for many seasons. You have been both faithful and kind, and those are uncommon virtues in one so young in years. I am proud of you, and I will miss you." Samuel started to interrupt, but Caleb would not allow it. "Our time together is like my basket. I know that you found great pleasure in our fireside conversations and that you regret there have not been more of them. But those long talks are like the large stones in my basket. They have filled some of our time together. Our long walks, our silent days and weeks, our wordless communion with the world and each other have filled the spaces around the talks. They have been our pebbles, our sand, and our water. Now, the basket is full."

Samuel pleaded, "Forgive me for my foolish heart. I have been impatient and unwise. I do not want to leave you, and it hurts me to think that I may have offended you. I am sorry."

"My young friend, you have nothing to be sorry for. This day has been drawing nearer to us since the day we first met. Today you will return to the Village. There, you will fill the basket of your life with love and marriage, the burdens and joys of parenthood, and the ache of grief and loss. Life deals these great passages to the fool and the sage alike. True wisdom, Samuel, belongs to those who can fill the empty spaces between life's great events with meaning."

Samuel buried his face in his hands and sobbed. When he was finally able to dry his eyes, Caleb was gone, as he knew he would be.

We all sat still until Haleigh clapped her hands and broke the spell her story had woven. The children scrambled to their feet. Zachary pecked me on the cheek and raced off after them. Haleigh and I worked in silence for the rest of the afternoon.

On my way home from the garden, I took a path that wound through the village and the forest. I stopped to watch groups of children playing Tee-Ho-Nan in the village, and I sat down on the bank of a stream in the forest and let my mind wander. I bathed my senses in the sounds, smells, and sights of a forest in its late afternoon glory.

Before he left with the herd, Bill and I had been piecing our thoughts together. We accepted the fact that we had spent our lives foolishly in the Other World. We saw that we had always been on our way to the next great event. Whether it was a Ph.D., a board certification, or finishing The Book, the goal was always more important than the moment.

We never thought about empty spaces in our lives because we never knew they existed. Haleigh's story this afternoon has taught me that filling a life with meaning is something like filling a belly with food. When human beings have enough food to lose their fear of hunger, they divide into two camps. Some eat to live; others live to eat. In the Other World, Bill and I had enough food, or great events, in our lives. We didn't need to worry about hunger, so we didn't look for nourishing food. We ate junk food. We filled our lives with unending work. We could just as easily have filled them with drugs, alcohol, television, gambling, exercise, or shopping, as others have. There are many THINGS in the Other World to occupy us. We pawned the ability to furnish ourselves with the joys we loved most as children—home, companionship, the wonder of the world around us—for predigested, shrink-wrapped, artificially colored bites of life that we thought were full meals.

The more at home I become in the village, the more I realize that our homes and communities in the Other World have fallen into disrepair. We don't realize they are a part of our joy. We are so used to THINGS, we don't always remember that love, affection, and joy are fleeting and difficult to find. We settle for counterfeits, fakes, because they are quickly purchased and briefly filling.

In the story, Caleb said, "True wisdom belongs to those who can fill the empty spaces between life's great events with meaning." I am going to teach myself how to do that.

> Meaning is the food and water that nourishes the human spirit. It strengthens us. The counterfeits of meaning tempt us with hollow promises. In the end, they always leave us empty and alone.

The Soul Stealer

LIKE MOST OF THE EXTRAORDINARY DAYS in our lives, this one provided no warning that it was going to be different. It made the shipwreck seem like a swim in a pond. From it I learned some sad truths about my training as a physician.

Jude was up early because she wanted to get a head start on turning the compost. Shortly after she left the cottage, I made my way to the barn and had the herd on its way to the meadow while the dew was still on the grass. The day passed uneventfully. I was more than halfway back to the barn in the late afternoon when I heard a child calling to me. It was Zachary. I could see him clambering up the path as fast as his legs could carry him. I trotted down to meet him halfway. His message stopped me dead in my tracks.

116

"Jude's sick, really sick," he told me, trembling with fear. "Hannah says you've got to come right away."

I put Zachary in charge of the herd and bolted down the path. My lungs burned as I sprinted toward our cottage. I crossed the porch in two bounds and crashed through the front door.

Hannah was standing at the window, her back to me. Jude was in bed. Her skin was as pale as the cottage walls. A cold sweat had drenched her tunic and left her hair damp and matted. She took shallow, irregular breaths. I felt for her pulse. It was so thin and rapid that I had trouble finding it. Her hand was limp and deathly cold. Her eyes stared blankly into the middle distance. She did not respond when I spoke to her.

"What's the matter? What's wrong? What happened?" I demanded. Hannah asked me to sit, but I said I could not sit until I got some answers.

Despite my protests, Hannah guided me to a bench by the fire pit and made me sit down. "Jude was working when she suddenly felt very weak," she said. "She fainted before Haleigh could get to her. Haleigh rolled up her sleeve and found this." Hannah pointed to an ugly brown ring with a bright red center on Jude's left forearm. "It is," Hannah went on, "the bite of a spider."

"You mean it's just a spider bite?" I jumped up. "You had me worried. This is going to pass, isn't it?" When

Hannah didn't respond immediately, I found myself asking, " It's going to be all right, isn't it?"

"This is an extremely dangerous bite," Hannah replied quietly. "It is the bite of the orb spider, the deadliest creature in all of Kallimos. We call it the Soul Stealer."

I didn't know what to say. A hand touched my arm gently. I looked down and saw Haleigh standing beside me, her face a grim mask. There was a basket filled with heart-shaped flowers by her feet.

"These flowers are the best available treatment for the Soul Stealer's bite," Hannah explained.

"That's all you've got?" I exploded. "Are you out of your mind? Jude's sick, and all you have to heal her with is a bunch of flowers? Save them for someone's funeral. We've got to do something."

Hannah and Haleigh did not reply. Instead, they set to work making a poultice from the flowers.

"This isn't medicine—it's herbal hocus pocus," I ranted. "You're going to let Jude die. That poultice is good for nothing, and you know it. She needs more. She needs an anti-inflammatory, a steroid, an antibiotic, an anti-venom. She needs an IV. Can't you see she's in shock?"

As Haleigh applied the poultice to her arm, Jude let out a low groan. If anything, she looked worse than she had before. I felt dizzy, and my knees started to buckle.

Hannah guided me back to the bench. Blood pounded in my ears. I continued my pleadings, albeit at a lower volume. "Hannah, Haleigh, you know how much I love her. I'm begging you to do everything for her. Spare nothing. I know you mean well, but one lousy poultice isn't enough. There must be more you can do." Jude muttered anxiously. I listened but could not make out what she was saying.

Hannah looked me straight in the eye. "William, there are times when doing too much is more dangerous than doing too little," she said. "This is one of those times."

"I don't know what you are talking about," I answered angrily. "I don't really care, either."

Hannah took my hands into hers. "Sit with her. Be with her. She needs you now as much as she needs our poultice. Hold her hand, and let her know you're here. Tell her that you need her and that she cannot let the Soul Stealer take her away from you."

I started to object but gave up. They were right; that was what I needed to do. It was all I could do.

119

Hannah lit a candle while Haleigh checked the poultice. It was dark outside. The village was silent. No children laughed. No voices sang.

Hannah, Haleigh, and I sat beside Jude as the night deepened. She slept fitfully. I watched every rise and fall of her chest, wondering if each breath would be her last. As a physician, I had often attempted to reassure family members as they sat beside the bed of a dying loved one. Now I was the one in need of comfort.

I prayed feverishly. I made a raft of far-reaching promises and improbable bargains. I wallowed in self-pity, imagining my life without Jude even before she was gone. I held her hand, placed cool washcloths on her brow, and kissed her as softly and lovingly as I knew how. I remembered the excitement of our early love. I remembered the swell of pride I felt when I watched her across a crowded room. I remembered how we dreamed of having children. She was my love, my life.

I know that I looked up at Hannah with that same look of pained confusion I had seen on the faces of so many husbands and wives, sons and daughters, fathers and mothers. I had answered those looks with complex, clinical status reports. Hannah answered mine with a single command: "Tell her what is in your heart."

With that simple permission, I poured out my soul to Jude. A door swung open inside me, and I held nothing back. I did not notice when Hannah and Haleigh left. I held Jude in my arms. Never has an embrace meant more to me. The hours passed—one breath, one caress at a time.

The sound of birds singing preceded the dawn. I thought about how much Jude loved the birds on Kallimos, how she would stop what she was doing and close her eyes so that she could drink in their song. Hannah returned and wordlessly changed the poultice. The soft light that comes with the dawn fell across the bed. Outside the cottage, I could hear hushed, half-hearted conversation and activity.

At last Jude stirred in her sleep. My heart leapt into my throat. She coughed and swallowed hard. I rearranged the pillows under her head and waited. Another hour passed. Then the quiet was broken by a tentative knock on our door. It was Zachary. He was carrying a bundle of wildflowers. He approached cautiously and laid them next to Jude. They filled the room with their perfume. He looked up at me as if asking permission to touch her. "Go ahead," I told him. He bent down and kissed her hand. Jude's eyelids fluttered and then opened. She looked at Zachary and then at me. Her eyes came alive and smiled at us.

I doubt that Zachary's feet touched the floor on the way out. He called for Hannah as he raced across the green. I cried hot, happy tears. My Jude was back. She had denied the Soul Stealer its prize. Hannah came bustling in with more of the heart-shaped flowers. She could not contain her joy.

"This is just as it should be. She is going to be all right. She is going to be fine." She fixed a pot of tea, helped Jude drink a bit of it, and then turned her attentions to me. "You also have had a difficult time of it, William. You need some rest. Go to my cottage and lie down." I started to protest, but Hannah would have none of it. "Haleigh and I will be with her. You have done your part, and you will have more to do later, but right now you need sleep."

I felt Jude squeeze my hand softly, once then twice. It was our secret sign that she agreed with what was being said. After a kiss and a hug, I was off to Hannah's place and sweet, dreamless sleep.

Jude gained strength slowly over the next several days. Haleigh, Hannah, and I took turns nursing her. One afternoon, while Jude was sleeping, Hannah and I sat together on our front porch. We had been talking about nothing important when she suddenly turned to me with a puzzled look. "I've been wondering about something, and I'd like to ask you about it," she said.

Her approach startled me. Always very open and direct, it was strange for Hannah to ask permission before venturing into a topic of conversation. "You have told me that you spent many years studying to be a physician. You seem justly proud of your hard work, which I can understand. Nevertheless, something worries me." I nodded encouragingly. "Were you never taught that the proper use of remedies is just one piece of the healing art?"

"I'm not sure what you mean."

"When Jude fell ill, I told you that it is sometimes dangerous to do too many things. You did not seem to understand me. I suspect that the healers of the Other World often substitute action for understanding. You must learn the story of Kahlid the Kind."

Hannah got up from her chair and went inside to check on Jude. When she returned, she settled herself into her chair in such a way that I knew a story was coming.

Long ago, when The People were still new to this world, a man lived with his family at the southern edge of the Great Desert in the village of Tum-Bak-Tee. Like his father and his father before him, he was a desert trader. Twice each year, once in the spring and once in the autumn, the trader would pack up his wares and harness his camel for the trek north to Mar-Kasha. Because he was a man of modest means and could not afford a caravan, he traveled alone.

Journey after journey, year after year, all was well. Then, one year, things went terribly wrong. As was his custom, the trader ventured north in the spring and, for the first eight days, made steady progress on the road to Mar-Kasha. On the morning of the ninth day, however, a wind began to dance across the desert. At first it was little more than a breeze, but it came from the west. The trader knew well that many deadly storms had grown from just such a wind as this.

The wind gained strength, lifting the scalding sand into the air. The trader's fear grew. Then the wind became an enormous black cloud of angry sand. It bore down on the trader and tore at his flesh. It lashed his faithful camel like a thousand braided whips. The beast stopped and refused to advance. The trader tumbled from his wailing beast and crawled to a nearby dune. There, he dug a pit and crawled into its depth. Above him, the wind howled its unending song of fury and pain.

By the time the morning light came, the storm was spent, and the trader unearthed himself from his hiding place. He searched frantically for his supplies and his camel. They were lost. He looked for the road to Mar-Kasha. It, too, was lost, erased by the power of the storm. He scrambled up the nearest dune and surveyed his surroundings, but all he saw was a boundless ocean of sand. Thinking a different view might give him some hope, he descended from that dune and climbed another. The scene was the same. All the while, the sun rose higher in the sky. Soon the trader's tongue cried for water, but he had none. His stomach pinched with hunger, but there was no food. That night, he shivered under the desert's cold canopy of stars.

When morning came again, his lips were cracked and his tongue was swollen. He thought of his family and how much they needed him. He forced himself to climb one more dune. When his eyes found only sand, he knew that his life was nearly over.

What the unfortunate trader did not know—in fact, what he could not know—was that the Oasis of Kahlid the Kind lay just one hour's walk to the east. Kahlid's Oasis was blessed with the finest, purest water in the desert, and Kahlid was famous for possessing the most generous heart the desert had ever known. Kahlid regularly rode the dunes in search of the lost and the forsaken.

Just as the trader prepared to close his eyes for the last time, Kahlid discovered him. Kahlid climbed down from his mount. He picked the trader up in his powerful arms, laid him across his camel's back, and rode swiftly home.

Back at the Oasis, Kahlid offered the trader water. The man drank deeply. Again and again he drank. At last, the water had answered his thirst, and the trader was able to speak. "You must be Kahlid the Kind," he croaked. "You have saved me when Death held his hand upon my throat."

Kahlid answered, "It was the will of God that you should live. Now drink; drink more, for surely you've not taken enough."

"I am grateful to you, but I have taken my fill of water. Now I feel a great hunger, and I'm tired. Might I have something to eat and a place to lie down?"

"Food? How can you think of food?" Kahlid thundered. "Not so long ago, you were nearly dead of thirst. Drink!" With that, Kahlid held up the skin of water. The trader turned his head away, and the water spilled to the ground. This action convinced Kahlid that the desert sun had addled the trader's mind. Wasting no time, Kahlid again picked up the trader. With the trader firmly in his grip, he waded into the cool, fresh water of the spring.

Once he reached its deepest spot, Kahlid began to dunk the trader's head into the water. The man thrashed and struggled, choking and gasping. He swallowed great gulps of fresh water. Kahlid was pleased. Over and over, he plunged the trader's head into the water. Finally, the man's strength began to wane. This alarmed Kahlid greatly, so he held him under for longer and longer periods to ensure that the man would drink.

In the end, the trader's strength dwindled to nothing. Death took him. Tears streaked the face of Kahlid the Kind as he carried the trader's still warm body from the spring to a place just outside of the Oasis. There Kahlid dug a shallow grave and laid the man to rest. He said the necessary prayers and covered him with sand and stones. This was not the first body laid to rest by Kahlid the Kind. When he was finished, Kahlid returned to the Oasis. There, he harnessed his camel and rode out into the desert heat again, muttering as he went, "Water, they must have water."

The story hit me hard. Hannah was right; I had been trained to see my work just as Kahlid the Kind saw his. I had been far more concerned with treatment than with the person being treated. Kahlid did not bother to listen to those he rescued because he was sure that they were thirsty. He saw the spring at his oasis as the answer to every problem he faced. He saved the lives of those he rescued from the desert, but they paid the highest possible price for this rescue. They drowned in the water that had saved them. My training and the training of all the other varieties of health-care professionals in the Other World had taught us to operate in the same way. The pills, potions, and therapies we had been trained in worked. They saved lives. But they could also kill.

With her story, Hannah showed me that the science of treatment should be the servant of care and never its master. The artful healer combines the physical treatment with true understanding of the one being treated.

I can see now that Jude owes her life to the wisdom of Haleigh and Hannah, whose caring allowed them to resist my demands to "do everything." Given Jude's fragile condition, my everything-plus-the-kitchen-sink approach to treatment could easily have killed her. They knew the best treatment to apply for the Soul Stealer's bite. They prepared the poultice correctly and changed it regularly. In their wisdom, they knew to show me how to care for Jude. She needed my love and tenderness. They helped me touch my soul to hers.

Medical treatment should be the servant of genuine human caring, never its master.

King Aeon's Feast

The first quarter of the moon ~

THE NIGHTS ARE COOL NOW, and Hannah says that the first frost will come soon. It is harvest time, and the village buzzes with unaccustomed activity. Jude has fully recovered from the Soul Stealer's bite and is stronger than ever. She and Haleigh are in the garden at first light and remain there until dusk. Everyone is working hard. Everyone is looking forward to King Aeon's Feast.

I was born in October, and I figure that one of these days was or will be my birthday. I'm not expecting a party. In fact, the idea of being in your twenties or forties is alien to the people of Kallimos. In the Other World, numbers like 5, 16, 18, 21, 40, 65, and 100 mark important milestones. Here, life events aren't tied to an age in years. In fact, no one here reckons their age in years. There are just three kinds of people in the village—children, adults, and elders. As soon as they are able to walk and speak, children are woven directly into the fabric of life. They work, play, sing, and laugh. Whether in the garden, in the goat barn, or at the loom, all children have chores for which they are responsible. Their work is balanced with play. The people say that play makes a child grow, and the sound of children playing fills the village throughout the day.

Adulthood begins when a young person leaves the family home and establishes his or her own home and family. The adults of Kallimos play less and work more than the children, but at the same time, it is not unusual to see adults playing alongside children during the middle of the day. Music is important here. This is good. Now I sing while I work. I never sang while I was at work in the Other World.

The last age is elderhood. The wisdom of the elders is the glue that holds the village together. In the Other World, the elderly often feel overwhelmed and afraid of the people and things that surround them. It is different here. Here, elders instruct adults and children in the art of living. Elders tell and interpret the stories, fables, and legends of Kallimos. These stories educate, inspire, and entertain. Frail and demented elders hold a special place of honor. They are believed to be the most human of all people on Kallimos.

The notion of honoring people with dementia seems strange to me. I was taught to see them in terms of what they have lost. After all, losing one's memory is the result of chronic, irreversible brain damage. How can we possibly honor brain damage? The people here believe that what we call dementia is a cleansing or a purification. Demented elders are purely themselves—they travel backward and forward through time in a way that the rest of us can achieve only in dreams. For the people, this is magic, and all such magicians hold honored places here.

Becoming an elder is a gradual process and involves many factors, not just age. When a man or a woman who is advancing in years begins to display the patience, tolerance, and wisdom of an elder, he or she may be asked to tell a story during a feast or holiday. Requests for advice and counsel come to those who earn their neighbors' esteem. Here, elders are consulted about all of life's major decisions. Young men and women ask their elders about everything, from their compatibility with a particular suitor to the number of children they should have. The advice they receive is not binding, but only a fool would ignore the wisdom of those who have already lived so long and so well.

Now, onto King Aeon's Feast. When I first heard about it, it sounded like a crazy, upside-down Halloween. There is nothing really like it in the Other World. It is celebrated on the first day after the first full moon following the harvest. On the night before the feast, every member of every household in the village dons a jet-black robe that covers him or her from head to toe. They place three empty baskets on their front porch, and then they fill three sacks—the first with potatoes, the second with tomatoes, and the third with corn. Their preparations complete, they slip outside and, dodging the moonbeams, place a potato, a tomato, and an ear of corn in each of their neighbor's baskets.

The following morning, all of the front-porch baskets are full, the black robes are gone, and the mood is festive. Everyone gathers on the village green and feasts on delicious sweet and spicy treats. The tables set up on the green groan under the weight of food, cider, and wine. Music fills the air, everyone dances, and no one works. The celebration lasts well into the night. The whole business sounds very strange to Jude and me. First, the people of Kallimos have no king, royalty, or ruling elite. Why would they celebrate a king? Second, donning camouflage and sneaking around in the dark is unlike everyone here.

A couple of days before the feast, I mentioned to Hannah that I didn't understand the purpose of King Aeon's Feast. "Come to me after the goats are down for the night, and I will tell you about King Aeon," she said.

The sun was low in the sky when I went to see Hannah. Jude was still in the garden, and I was glad for Hannah's offer of company. We watched the dark red sun sink below the sea's horizon. The evening air was cool. We covered ourselves with a quilt and talked as we waited for the stars to appear. The people of Kallimos say that the stars do not shine during the day because they are afraid of the sun. Even when they show themselves in the night sky, they tremble with fear, which is why they twinkle.

In my mind, I know that the stories of Kallimos are just fantasies. In my heart, though, I believe every word of them. The stories bind me to this place, to this way of living, and to the world in a way that science never did. In the Other World, science always has some new breakthrough that shows we are completely wrong about what we think we know. Then, just when we come to accept the new breakthrough, it is itself disproven. Knowledge always changes. Wisdom is different, and the wisdom in the stories here is constant. I like that.

Finally, when all light had faded from the west, Hannah began the story of King Aeon.

Long ago, when The People were still new to this world and did not understand the wisdom of the

Elders, a male child was born into the Village. When his mother and father first heard his lusty cry, they knew that he would grow into a powerful man. For this reason, they named him Aeon, which means "the one who calls on the wind to obey."

As Aeon grew to manhood, he dreamed of becoming king of all The People. He gathered his followers around him and convinced them to turn against the Village. He showed them how to cut oak branches and sharpen them into deadly spears. Then, with his men and their weapons by his side, he marched against The People.

"Hannah," I interrupted her, "stop."

She waited for me to speak.

"This is what I've been worried about. The village is completely defenseless. I've been meaning to bring this up with you for a while. We've got to get organized, or one of these days we're going to find ourselves at the mercy of someone just like Aeon."

Hannah replied confidently, "That day will never come."

"It could."

"It will not. We are safe here. You just do not recognize our defenses."

"Don't try to humor me," I said sharply. "Nothing is being done about this."

"We possess nothing that anyone would want. All of our wealth lies in our hearts. It cannot be stolen. Now shush and listen to the story."

Aeon's warriors threatened every man, woman, and child in the Village. "Aeon is your master now," they cried. The People trembled with fear. In less than a day, Aeon conquered the Village and declared himself king. "But surely," he thought, "a king should have a palace. A king should be rich, much richer than the commoners over whom he rules."

In the first year of his reign, as spring approached, he issued a proclamation: "I will divide this year's harvest with my subjects according to the following rule. I will take for myself the tops of all that is grown. Commoners may content themselves with the bottoms." The People shuddered when they heard this. How would they survive?

"That's just what I mean, Hannah," I broke in again. "We don't have much, but even a little bit is enough to attract the attention of a predator like Aeon."

"We have nothing to fear," she said, and went on with the story.

The oldest member of the Village was a woman called Emma. In the past, when Emma was younger and still working her garden, many in the Village had sought her advice. Emma's garden had been lush and green, and because of the bounty she brought forth, she was held in high esteem. In time, however, the many seasons of Emma's life took the strength from her, and Emma retreated from her garden. In time, she was nearly forgotten.

Now, as the members of the Village worried over King Aeon's proclamation, they thought of Emma. Many doubted that she could survive the privations that would result from King Aeon's decree. After much discussion, the members of the Village went to Emma with great sorrow to tell her of Aeon's proclamation. They found her sitting alone by the fire. Crumpled by her years, she did not look up when they entered.

Emma listened to their words and then folded her hands and looked into the fire for a long time. Finally, she spoke, her voice barely more than a whisper. "My children, my grandchildren, do as I say and all will be well. When the sun warms the Earth and it is time to plant your crops, sow your gardens with these things only: turnips, potatoes, onions, garlic, rutabagas, peanuts, and carrots. When the harvest comes, give to Aeon what he has demanded and keep for yourselves what he has bid you to keep."

The People listened to Emma and did as she said. When the harvest was in, cart after heaping cart of shriveled carrot tops and rotting potato vines were delivered to Aeon and his young soldiers. Meanwhile, The People filled their own cellars with the bounty of the harvest. During the long winter that followed, the young soldiers grumbled with every bowl of carrot-top soup.

The following spring, Aeon was determined not to repeat his error. "This year," he declared, "I will divide the harvest with my subjects according to the following rule: I will take for myself the bottoms of all that is grown. Commoners may content themselves with the tops."

Again, King Aeon's words stirred fear in the hearts of The People. Certain that this new royal proclamation would destroy them, The People gathered in Emma's house and shared the terrible news with her. Emma welcomed them to her home and listened as they told her of Aeon's command. She looked deep into the fire. Then she said, "My children, my grandchildren, do as I say and all will be well. When the sun warms the Earth and it is time to plant your crops, sow your gardens with these things only: peas, beans, tomatoes, broccoli, and peppers. When the harvest comes, give to Aeon what he has demanded and keep for yourselves what he has bid you to keep."

Again, The People listened to Emma and did as she said. When the harvest was in, cart after heaping cart of tangled, dirty vegetable roots were delivered to Aeon and his young soldiers. Meanwhile, The People filled their own cellars with the bounty of the harvest. The young men muttered and snarled as they choked down the bitter, stringy roots three times every day all winter long.

By the following spring, Aeon was well aware of the anger and resentment that lay coiled within his army. His foolish subjects had somehow managed to get the better of him the past two years, but this year, he said, would be different. He pondered the problem for several days and then declared, "This year, I will take both the tops and the bottoms of all that is grown. Commoners may content themselves with the middles."

King Aeon's words drove The People to the edge of panic. Surely the end was near, they thought. There was no way they could give Aeon the tops and the bottoms of all that they grew and still have enough to survive. Not even Emma could save them from this, and it was with heavy hearts that they went to tell her of their impending destruction.

Emma listened as they repeated the King's command. She put her chin in her hands and closed her eyes. The People watched, waited, and listened. She wandered in and out of the seasons of her life. She sighed deeply, and then she thought some more. Still they waited, hoping for a miracle. She looked deep into the past. Finally, she said, "My children, my grandchildren, do as I say and all will be well. When the sun warms the Earth and it is time to plant your crops, sow only corn in your gardens. When the harvest comes, give to Aeon what he has demanded and keep for yourselves what he has bid you to keep."

When the harvest was in, cart after heaping cart of brown, withered cornstalks were delivered to Aeon and his young soldiers. Meanwhile, The People filled their own cellars with the bounty of the harvest. When they saw Aeon had been outsmarted a third time, the soldiers raced through the palace with their swords in hand, looking for the king, but they could not find him. The cruel king had seen the cornstalks rolling toward his camp and understood the fate that awaited him. He escaped into the forest and was never seen or heard from again.

Thinking Hannah's story was finished, I said rather patronizingly, "That's a clever tale, but what if Aeon hadn't been so patient? What if he had just killed everyone?"

Hannah turned to look at me. "Where did you ever get such a dark imagination?"

"I'm afraid to tell you that it happens all the time in the Other World. Madmen kill whole nations. They're so full of hate they can't think of anything but the wrongs they think have been done to them. They'd think nothing of destroying a peaceful place like this."

"The story is not finished," was Hannah's reply. "Listen to what happened next."

When The People learned that Aeon had fled, they turned their anger on those who had served him. They collected into an angry mob and, hungry for revenge, marched on the palace. They surged forward and then stopped. Emma stood alone in front of them. She cast her eye upon them, and slowly the crowd grew quiet. At last, she spoke, "The young men who sided with Aeon have done you wrong, and now you seek their blood. They were fools, but who among you has not played the fool? They were wrong, but who among you has not been wrong?" A wave of grumbling and cursing swept through The People. Emma silenced them with her loud, clear voice. "If blood is what you seek, then you might as well take mine. There will never be a place for an old woman like me among people with hearts as hard as yours."

A young woman's voice rang out, "Tell us more."

Emma continued, "The followers must be forgiven and taken back into the bosom of the Village. If you strike these men down, the blood they shed will stain your hands and the hands of all The People for a hundred generations to come." They listened to Emma the

Elder, and her courage and wisdom filled the air around them. The People breathed it in, and it changed them. Finally, she said, "My children, my grandchildren, do as I say and all will be well. Prepare a great feast and make places at your tables for the young men who followed Aeon. Feed them, sing for them, and dance with them. Show them the wisdom of the Village and the foolishness of kings."

That is how the celebration of King Aeon's feast came to be.

"It makes much more sense now that I've heard the story," I said. "It's a reenactment of Emma's outwitting of King Aeon. The celebration that follows keeps the lesson of forgiveness alive and also reminds everyone that no matter how powerful a ruler may be, the village, under the guidance of its elders, is wiser and more enduring. It's a good philosophy, Hannah, but I'm afraid it wouldn't work in the Other World. The elders there have started more than their fair share of wars. In fact, some say that old men are far too willing to send young men to their deaths.

As Hannah sat lost in thought, the smoke from the village fire drifted our way, carried by a light breeze. Candlelight lit the windows of the cottages surrounding the green. "The problem is not with the elders," she said at last. "It is with the lack of honor they are finding in

141

their latter years. When an elder is held high in the esteem of his village despite his failing body, he gains the confidence to speak with wisdom. The honor and well-being of the village become more important than any other consideration. When an elder is seen simply as a weaker, slower, less able version of his younger self, he naturally seeks to regain what he has lost. He tries to act and think like the young and, thus, gives poor counsel to the village. When the young fail to honor the aged for what they are, the wisdom of the elders cannot bloom."

Hannah's words moved me to make a confession. "I've always thought of the elderly as weaklings in need of protection. I was most interested in the things they had lost and what they could no longer do. I have a hard time thinking of them as guardians or protectors."

Hannah replied, "More than anything else, they protect us from the destruction that can be wrought by the misguided passions of youth."

I grunted, "That's very nice, but the village needs a real defense if it is going to be safe from an invader."

"I'll tell you what—if I can give you an example of the protective power of the elders' wisdom, will you let go of your concerns about our safety?"

"I will," I answered, "but only if it is a real example and not just a story."

Hannah's face broke into a mischievous grin. "I assure you that this really happened."

"Go ahead, then."

"Not so long ago, a young man came to the village. Oh, he was so full of anger, and he cared nothing for the ways of the people. He was strong, smart, and powerful. It would have been easy for him to bring us under his sway. He could have ruled us as a tyrant."

I interrupted her again. "Yes, this is just the sort of thing I have been talking about. What good are the elders against a man like that?"

"The elders of the village looked into this man's heart, and they understood him. They brought calm to the storming waters of his soul. They loved him like a son and taught him the lessons of Kallimos."

I had to wait a long time before I could speak. "You're sitting next to that man right now, aren't you."

She looked at me and caressed my face with her hand. "I am," she said.

It was time for me to go. Jude would be waiting for me. I put my arms around Hannah and held her close to me. There seemed to be nothing more that I could say, and so I took my leave. The peace of the evening surrounded me as I walked home.

In a human community, the wisdom of the elders grows in direct proportion to the honor and respect accorded to them.

A Trip to Shah-Pan

The full moon waning ~

JUDE CAME HOME with exciting news yesterday. At least, I think it's exciting. Haleigh has decided to visit her sister, who lives in a village three days east of here, and has invited Jude to join her. The people of the village rarely travel, and Haleigh makes this trip just once a year. They will stay with Haleigh's sister for about two weeks. I have urged Jude to take my journal so she can describe the sights. She says she will.

Haleigh's sister lives in a village called Shah-Pan, which means "the place where the mountain gives birth to the river." The route Haleigh and Jude will follow runs alongside the Kwa-Na-Na River, which has me somewhat worried. Some say that tigers still prowl the banks of the river. I spoke at length with Hannah this morning about my concerns. She says that nowadays tigers prowl only in legends and stories. I sure hope she's right. She also suggested that some of my concern may be related to how much I will miss Jude while she is gone. Truer words were never spoken.

Jude leaves in the morning.

The new moon ~

I'm glad that Bill suggested I take his journal. There is something I very much want to record about this trip. Just eleven days have gone by since we set out on our journey, but it seems like a lifetime. This is the height of the rainy season, but Haleigh assured me that the weather would favor us. It did. We have been blessed with clear skies and pleasantly cool temperatures so far. To get to Shah-Pan, we followed an ancient footpath that skirts the bank of the Kwa-Na-Na River. The route starts out as broad and smooth as any village path. The farther it goes, though, the narrower and steeper it becomes. In the Other World, we would have lugged along bundles of equipment and supplies. Here, people travel light and live off the land.

On the first day, I fussed and worried like an old hen. I worried about having packed so little food. What if we ran out and had nothing to eat? Where would we sleep? What if the rains came? I knew Haleigh had made the trip many times, but the trail was unmarked and there certainly weren't any forest rangers to give assistance. What if she became confused and made a wrong turn? What if we got lost?

I barely slept that first night and awoke feeling groggy and out of sorts. I was beginning to regret my decision to come along. I'm sure Haleigh sensed my anxieties, but instead of telling me not to worry or making me feel guilty for doubting her, she began pointing out the edible plants and potential shelters that lay along our path. I was feeling much better when we sat down for our midday meal.

Out of nowhere it seemed, Haleigh brought forth from the wilderness the ingredients for a delicious pot of soup. I had just finished my meal when she sighed and looked up from her bowl. "I'm worried about you, Jude," she said. I started with surprise at her comment. I thought I had hidden my concerns fairly well. "We are now a day and a half from the village, and this afternoon we face the most difficult portion of our journey. You are young and strong, and I have no doubt that your legs can carry you to Shah-Pan. But I am not so sure that your spirit is ready."

"But, Haleigh," I said, "I'm really excited about seeing the village and meeting your sister. Really, I can't wait. From everything you've told me, I'm sure that it's very beautiful."

Her eyebrows knitted together briefly. Then, with a long, low groan, she pulled herself up from her place and started down the path, walking away from Shah-Pan. I caught up with her quickly.

"You're going the wrong way!" I said. She stopped and looked at me. I pointed up the path. "Shah-Pan is that way."

"I've decided not to go to Shah-Pan," she said stiffly. "I'm going back to the village." This kind of capriciousness was just like her, but here in the wilderness it scared me. All of my anxieties came rushing back. Haleigh continued down the path.

I stood there fighting my fears for a moment, and then it hit me. She was trying to teach me something, and I was being dense. I called out, "Stop. Wait for me. I'm coming with you." She stopped and waited for me to catch up. Together, we walked down to the edge of the river. "My dear, I am so happy that you have at last decided to join me," she said as we soaked our tired feet in the cool, rushing water. "I have been traveling this road alone."

I knew what she meant as soon as she said it. I had been consumed with worry ever since we had left the village. I had wanted the village's comfort and security. And when I wasn't worrying about what I'd left behind, I was fantasizing about the sights and sounds to come. Haleigh was right; the past and the future had squeezed out any possibility of enjoying the trip itself. "I'm here with you now," I told her.

"Good. I welcome you. It seems right to me that we should stay the night here. It is a good place, and we will have time to talk." The sun shone through the branches and warmed the stones on which we sat. "When you lived in the Other World, you let that which lies in the distance fill your sight. You grew timid and afraid of life. But now you are on Kallimos, and that means that you must learn to see the world as we see it. You must understand that the manner in which you search is as important as the thing you seek."

I nodded.

"Before we left the village, William asked Hannah about the danger we might face from prowling tigers. Well, the tigers left this part of Kallimos long ago, but we have a story about them that I think might help you now."

As far as I was concerned, Haleigh had just opened the doors to paradise. I could lie back in the warm sunshine and listen to one of her stories.

Long ago, when The People were still new to this world, there lived a young woman whom it is our duty to remember. Her name was Rachael, and she lived in a little village in the northwest corner of Kallimos. In the spring of the year, she fell in love with a handsome young man. His name was Henry, and he was tall, with powerful arms that understood hard work, and a deep voice that was accustomed to laughter. In the evenings, they strolled through the village arm in arm. The Elders nodded approvingly. "Yes," they said, "this is a good match." As the lovers walked, they talked of their love and the life they would build together. They talked of the children they would bring into the world and the names they would give them.

Soon, permissions were asked and granted. The date was set, and the announcement was made. All was well until two days before the wedding. On that day, the heat of the summer drove everyone inside, so they did not hear the thunder of hoofbeats until it was too late. Over the crest of the hill and into the village rode a great warlord with his army of thugs and bandits. They leaped from their horses and shouted that they would have all the young men for their battle with Mar-Kasha or destroy the village. Henry was dragged from his home and beaten until he was bloody. Then he was carried away.

Rachael screamed until she had no voice. She cried until she had no tears. But it was to no avail. Henry was gone. One spring came and went, and then another, and then another. Still, Rachael waited for her lover to return to her. It was in the spring of the fourth year that Henry returned. Word of his approach swept through the little village. The Elders asked the children to tell Rachael the news. They sang in joy to her, "He's

here, he's here, he's here! He's come back to you!"
Rachael ran down the road to meet him. When she
reached him, she threw her arms around him. Tears
flooded her cheeks and splashed on his tunic.

Henry's arms remained at his sides. He did not
speak to her. He did not look at her. He withdrew
from her embrace and trudged toward his parents'
home. All of the loneliness, the doubt, and the pain she
had suffered during the long years of their separation
were, in that instant, reduced to a single drop in her
ocean of anguish.

Well, as you know, permissions had been asked and
granted. Promises had been made, and so Rachael and
Henry were married. They made their new home in a
small cottage near the edge of the village. Henry was
up with the sun and remained in the fields until the
supper hour. He ate in silence and then went to sleep
on a straw mat beside Rachael's bed. Night after night,
Rachael watched him thrash in his sleep. She dared not
rouse him or even speak to him, for his eyes flashed
with a violence that made her tremble in fear.

Every day, as her dreams deserted her, Rachael died
a little bit. Finally, seeking to end her torment, she
resolved to visit the wise old woman whom her mother had told her lived in the forest above their village.
When the moon was full, Rachael crept out of the cottage and walked slowly along the twisting forest path

150

that led up the hillside. At last, she reached the wise woman's cottage. She knocked softly on the door. An ancient, wrinkled voice called, "Come in, come in."

The hinges groaned as she pushed the door open and stepped inside. A tiny old woman beckoned Rachael to join her beside a small fire. The dim light threw shadows into the corners of the room. The sage smiled and bid Rachael to speak. Rachael poured out her story. "What can I do?" she asked. "Am I destined to endure this burden forever?"

The sage smiled. "My dear, I have good news for you. There is hope. Yes, there is hope." The unhappy bride's heart sang with joy. "Bring me a tiger's whisker," the sage said, "and happiness will be yours."

Rachael's heart sank. "A tiger's whisker?" she asked, hoping that she had somehow misunderstood the words.

"Yes. Bring me a tiger's whisker, and I will show you how to put your woes behind you. Now, return to your home."

The walk down that forest path was long and lonely. How, Rachael thought, could she ever get a tiger's whisker? Attempting such a thing would mean certain death. It was an impossible request. There was nothing she could do.

A season passed, and Henry remained as cold to her as he had been on the first day of his return. One day, as Rachael sadly went about her chores, she heard her neighbors talking about a tiger that had come down from the mountains to prowl the riverbank at night. "Better to be devoured by a tiger than to endure this slow torture," she decided.

That evening, she slipped down to the riverbank and sought the tiger, but she did not find him. She returned the next night and the night after that. Finally, she glimpsed the orange and black as the cat walked along the riverbank. Her heart pounded, and her hands grew cold with fear. Still, she returned the next night and saw him again, walking along the river. Perhaps he is hungry, she thought. Early the following evening, she scattered a few bits of meat along the tiger's path and then retreated to the safety of the forest.

The tiger appeared at his appointed hour. He stopped, sniffed the offering, and devoured it before moving on. Every night, Rachael left an offering in the tiger's path, and each night she crept a little bit closer to where he stood and ate. Finally, after many long months, she stepped forward and laid her hand on the tiger as he ate. He growled ominously, and she froze, ready to be taken into his jaws, but instead the tiger turned and disappeared into the night. Each night from then on, Rachael would stroke the tiger as he ate. Finally, when the moon was full and the tiger was eating happily, Rachael reached down and firmly grasped a single whisker between her thumb and forefinger. Not daring to breathe, she pulled on it sharply. The tiger snarled once and then loped off toward the mountains.

She had done it. Clutching the tiger's whisker, Rachael walked home, never taking her eyes off the prize she held. By the light of their only candle, she placed it in a small, silken pouch. She tied the pouch to a string and placed the string around her neck. A hundred times during the next day, she fondled the little silk pouch. Finally, when night came and Henry lay deep asleep on the floor next to her bed, she raced up the forest path to the sage's cottage. Stepping onto the porch, she pounded on the door. "Are you there?" she cried. "I am here," the old woman answered. "You may enter." Rachael burst into the cottage. "I have done what you asked me to do. I have brought you a tiger's whisker."

"Let me see what you have." With shaking hands, Rachael gave the pouch to the sage. The old woman opened it, grasped the whisker, and held it up in the light of the fire.

"Why, it is just as you say. You have brought me a tiger's whisker. A fine one, too." The sage took one long, last look at the whisker and then tossed it into the fire.

Rachael shrieked and lunged toward the fire, but it was too late. The flames had already consumed the precious whisker. Between her sobs, she gasped, "You don't know what I had to do to get that whisker! And now it is gone!"

The sage massaged Rachael's shoulders until her grief was spent. At last, the sage spoke. "I know well what you had to do to get the tiger's whisker, and so do you. Go home now and be happy. Life will be good to you now that you have learned how to be its master."

Still weeping, Rachael left the sage's cottage and blindly began her descent to the village. Halfway down, she stopped to rest and wipe her eyes. In the darkness that surrounded her, she could hear the leaves on the trees rustle and an owl hooting deep in the forest. Still, she did not move from her resting place. Suddenly, the meaning of the tiger's whisker and the sage's words became clear to her.

Gathering her courage about her, she returned to the cottage and the man she loved. In time, she led him back to the love he had lost. Fortune blessed them with many children, and their years were long and full.

I said nothing when Haleigh finished the story. I wanted to think it over for a while. After supper, as we laid out our bedrolls, I brought it up. "That story, the tiger's whisker, it taught me something."

Haleigh turned toward me and said, "Then it did what it was meant to do. The story has been my friend through many dark days. It continues to teach me, even to this day."

I had a hard time imagining someone as wise as Haleigh still learning from a story she must first have heard as a child. It made me feel much less confident about the lesson I thought I had learned. I think Haleigh sensed this because she sat up and gave me her full attention. "Tell me, child, what did you learn?"

I drew a deep breath. "Before that story, I did not understand the relationship between patience and courage. In the Other World, courage is found in dramatic gestures and acts of bravery. The courage to be patient is something we rarely think of as courage. Now I can see that patient courage is the true courage. I've always wanted the next thing in my life to come to me NOW. I remember being a child and seeing my sister break out with pimples on her face. I wanted to have pimples on my face right then and there. I didn't want to wait. But, when they did come to me, I wanted them to go away."

Haleigh gazed into the fire and nodded. "When we left for Shah-Pan, you wanted to be in Shah-Pan. When we arrived, you would, no doubt, want to be home in the village."

"For a long time—my whole life, I guess—I've been living in a cage. I've been a prisoner to what comes next. You are trying to set me free, aren't you?"

"Yes, I would love to see you live the way a human being was meant to live."

Brimming with enthusiasm, I asked, "When can I start?"

Haleigh let out a rasping chuckle that escalated into a laugh. "My dear child, you begin right now, right here, in this moment. The only moment you will ever know, the present."

I laughed with her. "I will begin now, in this darkness, lying on this ground. When it is time to walk, I will walk; when it is time to laugh, I will laugh; when it is time to cry, I will cry. I am with you now, Haleigh, and I will remain with you."

"Those words are spoken like a true human being."

In the flickering light of our dying campfire, I could see Haleigh smiling. I crawled into my bedroll and watched the stars wink through the leaves overhead. "You once asked me," Haleigh said, "why we travel so

156

rarely. For us, the daily life of the village is its own jour-ney. We do not need to seek beauty or change in faraway places. It is with us all the time."

The smoke curled into the darkness above the dying embers. I snuggled down in my bedroll. Haleigh was pleased with me, and I was happy and tired.

Each day of our journey and stay in Shah-Pan, it seems to me now, has been filled with wonder. Never again will I separate the road that I travel from the thing I am seeking.

Human growth must never be separated from human life.

The Storm Warning

THOUGH THE FAMILIAR SOUNDS of the village fill the air outside our window, my thoughts are unsettled. Haleigh and Hannah came to our cottage in the middle of the night last night. They roused Jude and me from a deep sleep and insisted that we needed to talk. Hannah pulled up a bench on my side of the bed, and Haleigh sat next to Jude.

Hannah's voice quavered as she spoke. "William. Jude. Haleigh and I have witnessed a number of peculiar omens recently."

"They haven't been seen since the days of Sarop the Great," Haleigh added.

"They come from the days when humans moved between Kallimos and the Other World," Haleigh added.

Jude rubbed the sleep from her eyes. "What does this

158

have to do with us?" she asked, stifling a yawn. "Can't this wait till morning?"

"No," Hannah replied. "We have come because we think they may be telling us about your future."

I stumbled out of bed and hunted in the darkness for a candle. In the dim glow of the banked fire, I could see Hannah glancing nervously at Haleigh. Haleigh hesitated before picking up where Hannah had left off. "These omens suggest that someone will be leaving Kallimos and journeying back to the Other World."

I looked at Jude and back at Haleigh. "Maybe. But my question is Jude's question. Why are you telling us?"

It was Hannah who answered. "We believe that it will be at least one of you who will be making that voyage. We cannot tell if you will make the journey together, or if fate will separate you forever."

I drew Jude close to me. "Look," I said to Hannah, "I have great respect for your wisdom, but this omen business sounds pretty weak. Is some constellation off kilter or something?"

She began to speak quickly. "No, no, it's much more than that. There are legends that speak of a time of great trouble in the Other World."

Hannah stopped and then went on. "The legends say that the three plagues will consume the elders of the

159

Other World and will spread to the young. You can help . . ."

Jude cut Hannah off without a word of apology. "I don't care about your stories and legends. Go away, both of you. I don't care what your omens say. Bill and I are happy here. We belong here. We're staying. Nothing can make us go back." Her outburst was followed by a thick silence.

I was the first to speak. "These stories are myths and nothing more. We aren't going anywhere," I said, trying to soothe Jude. "We're safe. Let's get up, put on some tea, and hear this out."

Playing host to our uninvited guests seemed to calm Jude. Once the mugs of tea were handed around, Hannah continued her story. "According to the legends, when the need in the Other World was greatest, there would be a great storm, and a visitor from the Other World would be washed onto our shore."

"Wait a minute," I interjected, "you were found lying on the beach. Perhaps these signs mean that you're the one who will return to the Other World."

"For many, many years I thought as you do, William," Haleigh said. "I knew that Hannah was the daughter of a healer, and I feared that she would be taken from my side and returned to the Other World. But many years have passed. I know now that Hannah will remain in Kallimos."

160

"Do the stories say how the visitor will return to the Other World?" Jude asked Hannah.

"One legend foretells the coming of a second great storm." She paused. "It is said that the visitor will be drawn back into the sea. That's all we know."

Jude's natural optimism presented itself. "Well, it's really simple, then. The story says that the visitor will be taken into the sea. If Bill and I stay away from the shore, we have nothing to fear. From now on, neither of us is going anywhere near the beach, not even for turtle eggs."

"Sounds good to me," I said, "but I have one more question. Haleigh, you said you were concerned about signs. What signs? What do you know that we don't?"

Haleigh said, "The plants, animals, wind, and sky all tell us that a great storm is approaching Kallimos. It will be much more powerful than the one that brought you here."

"Oh." I breathed a sigh of relief. "So, in reality, you don't have any hard evidence. You're going on a hunch. This is really just a guess."

Hannah opened her mouth to answer my challenge and then seemed to think better of it. "I suppose you are right." Then, turning to Jude, she said, "We've kept you up long enough. The sun will be up before long. We'll be going now."

We walked them to the door and bid our farewells there. After they left, Jude went inside, but I lingered by the open door. Haleigh's voice came floating back to me as they crossed the green. "They still believe that their fate will answer to their will. They still have much to learn, but time is against them now. Soon we will mourn their passing from this world." I struggled to make out the rest of what she was saying. "When the time is nearer, be sure to teach them the story of the treasure seekers. It will serve them well in the Other World."

I crawled into bed and found Jude already fast asleep. My heart pounded against my ribs. *Soon we will mourn their passing from this world.* Haleigh's words would not let sleep come.

Full moon ∼
The weather has been fantastic. The blue skies are punctuated only by brief rain showers. No storm clouds on the horizon, and neither Haleigh nor Hannah has spo-

ken of omens or signs. Jude and I have attributed their midnight visit to superstitious beliefs that we don't and probably won't understand.

Waning full moon ∼

I came down from the Summer Hills today feeling as bright as the sun. On my way home from the goat barn, Zachary lured me into a game of hide and seek. Consequently, I was a little late. When I got to the cottage, I found Jude sitting on the front porch with a picnic basket at her feet.

"I thought you'd never get home. You were playing with the kids again, weren't you?"

"It was all Zachary's fault," I grinned. "No man can be expected to resist a game of hide and seek."

"Hannah invited us to her house for supper." Jude picked up the picnic basket and stepped off the porch. "I don't want to show up empty handed."

Her words stopped me cold. "Hannah asked us over? Why? Did she say why?"

My suspicion puzzled Jude. "It's no big deal. She just said it had been a long time since we'd been over and . . ."

"And what?" I demanded.

"And she had a new story to tell us. That's all."

Her words hit me like bricks. I didn't know what to say. I didn't want to admit to eavesdropping on our guests' conversation, and I didn't want to alarm Jude. I decided to wait and see what would happen. I told Jude that I'd wash up and be right with her.

The meal was delightful, as was the companionship. We laughed, told stories, and sang songs. And then Hannah brought out her sweet, hot, after-dinner tea, and we settled into our chairs. My heart was in my throat as she began her story.

Long ago, when The People were still new to this world, there was a small village high in the mountains. Five towering peaks surrounded it. The People called the village Neekells, which means "the palm of the hand of stone."

Still, for all of its beauty, Neekells had poor soil, and its air was thin and cold. It was only the stubbornness and unceasing hard work of the few dozen families who lived there that kept them from hunger and cold. There were stories of an older time, a time when Neekells was a thriving city, but that was long ago. Those were the days when miners swarmed the five peaks. They burrowed deep into the mountains, and the mountains rewarded their labor with gold, silver, and jewels. Now, all that remained of those times were the stories and the town hall. It was the most beautiful building in Neekells, and The People loved it.

One year, a disastrous summer storm swept down from the mountains. Wind, rain, and hail flattened the crops and tore the roof off the town hall. The rain poured into the gaping hole and flooded the building. Unable to repair the damage, The People gathered together to tear down what remained of their hall. They pulled down the walls and cut up the timbers, which they hoped to use for their fires during the long winter that lay ahead. At the end of the day, as they gathered for their meager supper, one of the children picked up the hammer her mother had been using and began to pound on the foundation's cornerstone. The stone rang with a hollow note. How could this be? The People wondered as the sound echoed through the ruins. Seizing a sledgehammer, one of the men split the stone open. Inside lay a letter, a map, and a compass. The letter was yellow and brittle with age. The man opened it carefully, and his eyes widened as he read it aloud.

"To The People of Neekells," he read. "We, the Elders, know that if this cornerstone has been wrested from its place, hard times have come to our village. We know well that the luxury the gold and silver have brought us will not last forever. It is right that we should plan for the future. Accordingly, we have set aside a chest of treasure for your use in this time of need. This is our gift to those who will walk these paths long after we are gone."

The remainder of the letter advised them to use the map and the compass to find the abandoned mine shaft that held their treasure. You can well imagine the joy of The People of Neekells. They were saved. The bleak winter would not starve them after all.

"Who shall we send?" The People asked each other excitedly. "Who will make the journey into the mountains?" After much discussion, The People decided to send Bruno, who was the tallest, strongest man in Neekells. A knapsack was filled with food and supplies, the map and the compass were put into Bruno's powerful hands, and everyone cheered as he strode out of Neekells toward the Five Fingers of Stone.

In just one day, Bruno climbed the narrow, twisting path that led to the deserted mine shaft. His heart leaped with joy when he saw the mouth of the tunnel, but as he stepped toward it, a gnarly, little, old man jumped out of the brush and blocked his path.

The hermit roared in anger, his voice ten times the size of his body. "Stop right there. You can turn around and go right back where you came from, you no-good trespasser. I know why you're here, and you're not going to get it."

Bruno snarled back at him. "You'll move if you know what's good for you, old man." Then he lunged at the hermit. The old man seized Bruno's arm and twisted it painfully behind his back. He spun the young man around and hurled him down the rocky path that led to the mine.

Bruised and battered, Bruno pulled himself up and charged the old man in a blood red fury. The hermit stepped calmly aside and tripped Bruno with his thick oak walking stick. Then he jumped on Bruno's back and started beating him about the head and shoulders. Bruno bellowed with pain, clambered to his feet, and ran down the mountain as if the devil himself were chasing him.

The People received Bruno's story with great concern. Now what would they do? They mumbled and frowned, they argued and discussed, until finally one voice rang out. "Let's send Lucinda. Lucinda can talk the bark off a tree."

Lucinda packed her knapsack, took the map and the compass into her hands, and left the village. It took her two days to scale the mountain and reach the path to the mine. As she approached the entrance, she spied the hermit loitering near the opening. Quickly, she ducked behind a tree, opened her canteen, and poured its contents onto the ground. Then she refastened the cap and stepped back out onto the trail. She hailed the hermit in her most cheerful voice, "Good morning, good sir." The hermit looked up, and she continued. "It is so delightful to see you, kind sir. I had thought that I was alone in the mountains, and now I know I am not."

To this, the hermit responded in the sweetest of tongues, "My dear, the pleasure is all mine, for it has been years since my eyes have rested upon such beauty." Lucinda smiled at his words. Bruno is such a fool, she thought. Force won't bring the treasure home, but sweet words will.

Lucinda wiped her forehead with the back of her hand and shook her empty canteen in front of the hermit. "I'm afraid I have run out of water. I hear a stream down below, but I'm so tired from my climb. Would you be willing to fetch me a canteen full of water?"

"I would be honored and delighted to carry out such a small task on your behalf," the hermit replied. "I'll get right to it." But then a frown crossed his face.

"There is just one thing, just one thing I do not, indeed, I cannot, understand."

"What is that?" Lucinda asked.

"I do not see how anyone could have allowed such a rare and gentle beauty as yourself to enter these wild environs unprotected. This is the season when the tigers that prowl these heights are mad with hunger. The danger is as great as your loveliness."

"Danger?" Lucinda exclaimed. She listened, certain that she heard the low rumble of a beast on the prowl. Anger welled up from deep inside her. The People of Neekells, she thought, had risked her life while they remained safe in their homes. She snatched the canteen from the hermit's hands, spun on her heel, and headed back to Neekells. It wasn't until she was down the mountain that her anger had cooled enough to reveal her folly.

The People of Neekells groaned when they saw Lucinda return empty handed. The snow clouds would soon be coming. Again, they gathered to discuss their plight. Again, they mumbled and frowned, talked and discussed, but this time to no avail. Finally, a creaky voice raised itself above the others: "I'll go."

The People turned, looked, and laughed. It was Virgil, the oldest man in the village. His back was bad, his hip was bad, and his hair was thin and white. If Bruno couldn't get the treasure, what chance would Virgil have, they wondered. Still, there was no one else.

"I'll go," Virgil said again, and with the greatest of reluctance, The People of Neekells stuffed Virgil's pack with food, handed him the map and the compass, and left him to head into the mountains.

It took Virgil three days to reach the abandoned mine shaft. He found it in the late afternoon, and the hermit was nowhere in sight. Virgil stopped by the side of the path, spread out his bedroll, gathered some firewood, and built a fire. He prepared a stew for the evening, and then sat back against the trunk of a tree and smoked his pipe.

At last, the hermit came crashing through the brush. "Another one, eh? I thought I was rid of the likes of you," he growled. Virgil took his pipe from his mouth, pointed the stem at the food he had prepared, and said, "Sit down, friend. You must be hungry."

"My stomach is no matter of yours," the hermit snarled.

"My stew never hurt anyone yet." Virgil leaned forward and ladled up a bowl of piping hot stew. The aroma made the hermit's mouth water.

"Well," the hermit hesitated, "I guess I might have a bit." He took the bowl from Virgil's hands. After the stew came a contented smoke on Virgil's pipe. After the smoke came a long, rambling conversation about old times, old people, and old ways.

Finally, deep into the night, Virgil said, "Old man, you have something we need, and we have something you need."

The hermit cut him off. "There's nothing you have that I need. Nothing."

"Sure, sure, so you say," Virgil acknowledged. "But the truth is something different. The truth is you need a home, old man, and we need the treasure. You come down the mountain with me and give us the treasure, and we'll make a home for you." The hermit snorted.

"I've made my offer, old man," Virgil said. "If it's a trade not to your liking, I'll leave in the morning and see that

170

you're never disturbed again." With that, Virgil crawled into his bedroll and fell into a much needed sleep.

The hermit was up at first light. "Come on, old man," he said to Virgil. "We're going down the mountain." Virgil yawned and stretched. By the time Virgil was up and moving, the hermit had pulled the treasure from the mine shaft. By the time the sun was fully up, the two men were on their way down the mountain.

The children saw them first. "Virgil's back," they shouted. The People flooded out of their houses and barns. They surrounded Virgil and the hermit and heaped them with praise.

With the treasure in hand, The People of Neekells bought the food they needed for winter. In the spring, they built a new town hall, a hall with a private apartment and a broad front porch. For many years, Virgil and the hermit sat on the porch and talked about old people, old times, and old ways.

Hannah's voice trailed off. I looked up and saw tears rimming her eyes. The flickering light of the candle made them glisten. Finally, she spoke again. "Life often leads us down unfamiliar paths. We come to places and decisions that we have not chosen for ourselves. Soon, life will ask you to fight the three plagues in the Other World, of that I am sure."

Jude wrapped both arms around me. "I thought we were past all that," she protested. "I thought we had agreed that Bill and I were going to stay here with you."

"That is what you decided," Hannah answered. "But our fates are more powerful than our desires. You will return to the Other World tomorrow, and you will go voluntarily."

Jude began to cry. As I rocked her in my arms, Hannah said, "My heart aches as well, for I love both of you, but you must learn this one more lesson before you leave Kallimos."

"I don't believe you, Hannah," I said. "I do not believe that we will leave of our own free will. I'll listen to your lesson, but only because I'll need it for my life here on Kallimos." Jude drew a deep breath, sat up straight, and dried her eyes. I nodded for Hannah to continue.

"We tell this story because it shows us the way of the sage as well as the path of the fool. You should think of the treasure of Neekells as the wisdom our ancestors have created for us.

"But why don't the people of Neekells have that wisdom?" I asked.

"Wisdom is not always laid at our feet. Sometimes, it is hidden away in the words people speak and in the things they do."

"But, if the hermit recognizes the treasure, why won't he share it?" Jude asked.

"The hermit represents all those who cannot see the difference between the way things are and the way they ought to be," Hannah replied. "Although his life is lonely and difficult, the hermit hoards the treasure. It is easy to see the error of the hermit's ways, and it is always tempting to act as Bruno acts. You have often spoken of men who believe force will bring them whatever they desire. You are more fearful of such men than you need to be. Their power can bring them many things, but nothing that lasts. They are foolish boys drunk on their own strength."

Jude answered her. "You don't know them, Hannah. They really are dangerous."

Hannah smiled, "Their force will always be met by force, and they will always be overcome."

"Live by the sword, die by the sword," I said.

"Yes, that's right, but remember that there are many kinds of swords. You will be tempted to pick up your own swords. Remember the lesson King Aeon learned at such a high price: Power and leadership are different things."

Jude understood Hannah's point. "We promise that we will never act like Bruno or Aeon."

"Your promise gives me comfort," Hannah said, "but it will be harder than you realize to keep your word on this."

"Now consider Lucinda," Hannah went on. "Lucinda represents those who think deceit and trickery

173

will bring them what they want. But the hermit recognizes her deceit and pays her back in kind.

"I know what you mean," Jude said. "People recognize hypocrisy. They mock it when they hear it, just as the hermit mocked Lucinda. Nothing changes, because people realize that the hypocrite's words are self-serving." Jude paused and then asked, "Who does Virgil represent?"

"Ah, yes, Virgil," Hannah answered. "Study him carefully and you will become wise in his ways. First, he promised only what he knew he could deliver. He simply said, 'I'll go.' Nothing more, nothing less. Second, he took his time. He waited for the hermit. He did not try to fill his pockets with treasure and disappear. Bruno and Lucinda saw the hermit as an obstruction, and that is how he acted. Virgil saw him as a human being, and so he acted as a human being. Third, Virgil offered the hermit a bargain: You give me something and I'll give you something. It was a trade, not a robbery."

"So, people should give because it is only after they give that they can receive," I concluded. Hannah smiled at me. It was a sad smile.

"Finally," she said, "remember this. Virgil kept his word. Virgil's honesty loosened the hermit's grip on the treasure, and when the treasure was shared, it served the hermit as it never had before.

"If we are unsure what to do, we'll think of Virgil, the

best treasure seeker of them all. We'll let the wisdom of Virgil guide us."

"Good—but it's just as important that you teach others these lessons as well. Teach them to use his example as a guide in their search for the treasure of ancient wisdom. Do this, and you will strike a mighty blow against the three plagues."

Jude took a deep breath and exhaled sharply, "Well, you've taught us something, Hannah. As usual, it was something important. The good news is that we'll get to put this lesson to work right here, because neither of us is going to leave Kallimos."

"That's right," I grinned, "you're stuck with us." I held up my teacup and gave a toast: "To lifelong friendship and many more suppers at Hannah's." In the fading light, it seemed to me that Hannah's cup trembled as she raised it to her lips.

It's late now. My candle is almost gone. The wind has picked up and shifted to the northeast. I can hear leaves skittering across the footpath to the center of the green. Fat raindrops are pattering on our roof. This is the last page in my journal. Tomorrow, I will have to ask Hannah for a new one. There is just enough room for her lesson.

Wise leadership is the lifeblood of any struggle against the three plagues. For it, there can be no substitute.

Zachary's Rock

THE WIND BLEW HARD THAT NIGHT when I finished my journal and crawled into bed. As dawn approached, the wind seemed to gather new strength. The banging of shutters woke me then, and I struggled to latch them. I remember how they rattled against their latches with an eerie, unsettled rhythm. I fell back to sleep, and then it was habit that woke us, not the sun. The weather meant there would be no trip to the pasture that day and no work in the garden. Jude and I ate breakfast together and washed it down with ginger tea without speaking of our dinner with Hannah.

After we finished, I dashed for the barn. The goats welcomed me and seemed reassured by my presence in the midst of the storm. I pitched fresh hay into their manger, filled their trough with water, and then set to milking. When I was done, I rechecked their provisions. The goats followed my movements with their eyes. I could see that they were aware of the rupture in the routine but happy to hide from the storm in this sheltered place. I lingered. I might have stayed with them all day, but a heavy rain began to beat menacingly against the walls and roof of the barn, and my thoughts turned to Jude. Whatever was to come, I thought, we needed to be together. I closed the door to the barn and dashed home through the wind and pelting rain.

Jude wasn't alone—Haleigh and Hannah greeted me as I bounded into the cottage. I changed into dry clothes and joined them around the fire.

"We thought the weather might be worrying you," Hannah explained. "So we decided to sit out the storm here."

The wind and rain pounded the sturdy walls of our home as we traded stories and jokes, as we sang and laughed. We spoke of the small, intimate things that make up life on Kallimos, that make up life everywhere. Hannah produced a crock of her delicious turtle eggs. They made a fine lunch.

It was after the dishes were washed and put away that Haleigh went to Jude and took her in her arms. She began to whisper in her ear. Jude began to sob. They held each other in a tight embrace. Then Haleigh came to me. She placed her hands on my arms, looked into my eyes, and said, "You are a fine man. No matter where the wheels of our lives take us, I will always remember you. You would honor me if you kept me in your heart as well. You would honor The People if you would tell their stories and teach others the lessons you have learned here."

She turned to face Jude. My tears choked me until I let them go.

Hannah came to me. She embraced me as she just had Jude and whispered into my ear, "Before the sun goes to the Moon, you will be in the Other World. You are a far different man than the one who was cast upon these shores. Then, you moved easily in the Other World. You understood it, and it understood you. Everything will be different for you now. You will long for Kallimos and loathe the Other World. You will try to hide from your pain. That is as it must be. When it is time for you to begin your work, I will come to you."

"No, Hannah," I wailed. "No. I can't go. I won't leave you." She held me while I cried like a child.

The east wind picked up strength. It moaned and rattled about our cottage. Jude and I clung to Haleigh and Hannah. We swore that nothing could make us move from this place. Nothing.

Coming to Kallimos, I realized then, had first broken, then healed me. I had arrived a man and had become a child. The people of Kallimos had shattered the hard shell that had encrusted my spirit. They had made me vulnerable and then had taught me the power of tenderness. I trembled at the thought of returning to a world against which I was no longer protected.

I watched Jude, knowing that she shared my fear. Nothing, I repeated to myself, could move us from our places. Nothing.

The front door of the cottage flew open, and Zachary's father tumbled in. He was drenched to the skin, and his face was white with terror.

"Is he here? Is he here?" he demanded, looking around wildly. "Zachary—is he here? I can't find him."

"What do you mean you can't find him?" Jude's eyes were wide with horror.

"We were together at home this morning, and then at midday I had to help a neighbor patch a hole in his roof. I told Zachary to wait for me and not go out, but when I returned he was gone. I've looked everywhere in the village. My boy is lost!" he wailed. "The storm has stolen him from me."

Before I could stop her, Jude was out the door and into the heart of the storm. I raced after her. The wind and rain pummeled my head and shoulders. The noise was deafening, and stinging drops blinded me as I tried to catch her.

Finally, I caught up to her and grabbed her arm. "I know where he is!" she shouted. "I'm going to get him. Tell everyone to meet me on the beach."

With that, she broke free from my grasp and disappeared into the storm. I pounded on the door of the first cottage along the path and yelled for them to tell everyone to come to the beach. Then I bolted from the house and ran to the beach, praying that Jude would still be there.

Jude was right. Zachary was there on his fishing rock. He'd known the storm would bring the big fish close to shore, and he had slipped out of his father's house hoping to impress all of us with a fish he would catch. He had not reckoned on the power of the storm when he waded out to his giant boulder. Now he was stuck. Unable to call for help above the roaring wind and unwilling to risk the surf that surrounded him, he sat there terrified. Jude plunged into the water. She was twenty yards ahead of me by the time I dove in after her.

The cold, white-capped waves towered over our heads, and the surf beat us relentlessly as we struggled to Zachary's rock. Jude reached it first and pulled herself up its slippery sides. I followed shortly after. At last, the three of us were together on the rock. We looked toward the shore. There, people were forming a human chain. Zachary's father, at the head of the chain, ventured into the roiling, waist-deep water. Together, they cut the distance of our return trip in half. Still, the storm surge was rising, and we needed to move. Jude and I took hold of Zachary's britches, waited for an incoming wave, and threw ourselves back into the churning sea.

We struggled to keep our heads above water. Twice the waves hurled us into the grasp of the waiting rescuers. Twice the undertow broke their grip. We were weakening quickly. Gathering our strength, we tried once more. We rode a wave toward shore and thrust Zachary into his father's arms. The powerful man held his son tight, but we lost our grip. The undertow pulled us back, this time more forcefully than ever. It drew us away from the shore and down, deeper and deeper into a frigid, terrifying world. At the last possible instant, we were shot upward as if out of the mouth of a cannon. The water changed from black to gray, from green to blue. A rolling breaker deposited us in shallow water. Together, we crawled out of the surf and collapsed on the coal-black sand.

The Other World

A BOOT IN MY RIBS roused me. I looked up into the narrowed, suspicious eyes of a Montserrat policeman.

"Hey, you, get up," he ordered. He used his foot to roll me over. I sputtered and spit the sand out of my mouth. The commotion roused Jude as well, and she sat up. We both looked at the policeman. He was a stout, weary-looking man with a stomach that hung a good six inches over his thick leather belt. "What's the matter?" he asked. "You two have a little too much to drink last night?" He chewed lazily on a toothpick. "Let me see your IDs."

We were still dressed in the clothing of Kallimos and, of course, had no papers and no valid explanation of where we had been or how we had come to be on this beach.

"We were in a shipwreck," Jude said hesitantly. "Our boat went down offshore here, and we lost everything."

The policeman looked skeptical and laid a hand on his billy club.

"Well, how about that. You both lost your IDs, your passports, and all your money." He looked at our outfits and my beard and said, "I think you're a couple of addicts all strung out with nowhere to go. You blew all your money and crashed here, right?"

I started to tell him about the rumblings we thought were the volcano and the way our boat had been torn apart. I tried to tell him that I was a doctor and Jude was a Ph.D. and that we'd been on vacation.

"The volcano's been quiet since February '89, a year ago now," he told us, "and I haven't heard any reports of a boat going down." Jude and I could only stare at each other. He reached behind his back and pulled out a pair of handcuffs. "I'm taking you in for vagrancy." He cuffed Jude and me together and pulled us to our feet. "Let's go."

The jail cell was small, furnished with only a rough wooden bench that stood against the back wall. The stench of urine was overpowering. Jude and I sat on the bench. Rational thought was beyond us.

We were questioned for several hours. The detective, who was clearly annoyed by us and our story, confirmed that a ship had gone down a year before in the location and manner we'd described. The bodies of the man and woman on board had never been found, and they had

been presumed dead. After we told him the same story with the same details at least a half dozen times, he called my parents' house. I'll never know how Dad stood the shock of that call. There he was, a father who had grieved the loss of his son and daughter-in-law, on the receiving end of a telephone call from a Montserrat police station. I can only imagine his emotions when the detective told him that his boy wanted to talk to him.

Dad confirmed our identities, which seemed to reassure the detective. Dad also promised to wire us money and make arrangements for a flight back to the United States in the morning. The detective seemed quite relieved to know we'd be leaving. Still, just to be on the safe side, he locked us in the drunk tank until Western Union called with word that our money had arrived. With that, he unlocked the door of our cell and swung it wide open, saying, "Out. And don't come back."

A driving rain met us as we left the building. A passerby said it was a 5-kilometer walk to the Western

Union office and gave us directions. One of the bars we passed was playing the song "Psycho Killer" at an ear-splitting volume. Somewhere past the bar, we could hear a man and woman quarreling. From an alley came the sound of children crying in frightened, screeching voices. At the Western Union office, we collected the money my father had sent and called a cab. We spent a long night at the airport.

I will remember the reunion with our families for the rest of my life. They met us at the Syracuse airport, and our homecoming was so emotional that even strangers at the gate got choked up.

The first week back is a blur. I remember our parents and brothers and sisters kept coming up and touching us as if they could not believe their eyes. They needed physical contact to verify what they saw. Visitors, many of whom we did not know well, streamed through my parents' house. At first, there were no questions. It was a miracle that we had returned, and that was all that mattered. As the days wore on and the stream of visitors slowed to a trickle, however, there was more time for our families to wonder what had happened. Where had we been? How had we survived? What was the story?

The initial questions were roundabout and very polite. We responded just as we would have if we had been sitting on the green in Kallimos. We spoke openly and without reservation. We told our families about Kallimos, its people, and their history, culture, and traditions. We spoke its language and told the stories we had learned there. We allowed the wonder in our listeners' eyes to drive us on and on. This was a mistake. Solid, commonsense questions were laid at our feet. Atlases were produced, and calculations were made. We must be mistaken, we were told. It was impossible. They gave us opportunities to change our story. They offered innocent-sounding alternatives to our wild yarn. All this from the people who loved us most. In our moments of privacy, we wondered what would happen if we told the truth to strangers. We decided not to find out.

Our families saw our stubborn insistence on the reality of Kallimos as proof of some hidden mental instability. There must have been a family meeting, because one day the whole subject was dropped, permanently. It was replaced by a concern for our future. When would we be getting back to work? Where would we live? How would we resume our careers?

Jude and I didn't know what we were going to do. Royalties from The Book had produced a sizable nest egg in our absence, but since we had been presumed dead, the publisher had assigned the second edition to a pair of professors from Southwest Texas University. Our apartment in New York was gone. We were homeless, jobless, and confused.

We started taking long drives through the counties in upstate New York where we had grown up. The early spring was beautiful, and driving aimlessly through the countryside gave us comfort. Then one day, we saw a hill that reminded us of one of the Summer Hills on Kallimos. We stopped the car and got out. There was a hand-lettered "For Sale" sign tacked to a tree at the edge of the road. Jude and I hiked to the top of the hill. There, we watched the sun slip slowly toward the horizon. We felt the land calling us home. Jude scribbled down the number on the sign, and in less than two weeks, all 211 acres were ours.

Life on Summer Hill

May 8, 1990 ∼

JUDE GAVE ME THIS JOURNAL tonight. The black cover reminds me of the one Hannah gave me, but this one has my name on the cover in gold letters. It's a lovely thing. Being back has been hard for both of us, and I think Jude realized that I needed some kind of release.

We've pitched a tent near the site where we'll build our home. We've built a fire pit and dug a latrine. In fact, the outhouse is Summer Hill's first permanent structure. We studied and restudied every potential home site, examining the light, the soil, and the drainage before we decided where to build. Today, we made the decision. The house will sit on the crest of the hill, facing south. Its back will nestle up against a hedgerow that should offer some protection against the winter's north wind. The soil here is deep and rich.

We've promised ourselves that we will live as we lived on Kallimos. This means doing without electricity, running water, and power tools. I'm afraid these eccentricities have confirmed our families' worst fears. They are certain Jude and I must have suffered blows to our heads during the course of our disappearance.

May 11, 1990 ∿

Jude and I have suspected it for several weeks, but today she went for the test. It's official—she's pregnant. The baby is due in December. If it's a boy, we will name him Zachary. If it's a girl, we'll call her Haleigh. Jude is sick in the morning but otherwise holding up well. We've told our families, and they are thrilled. It's the best thing that has happened to us since our return.

June 8, 1990 ∿

The black flies were deadly yesterday. They feasted on me, but they couldn't drive me off the roof. I drove the last nail into the last shingle this morning. Today, we moved out of the tent and into the house. Living in a house while it is being built may test our patience and persistence, but it beats the heck out of life in the tent.

With a baby on the way and no refrigeration, we are going to need a fresh supply of milk. I told Jude she is lucky she married a first-class goatherd. I've sketched out plans for a barn that will be smaller but just as serviceable

as the one on Kallimos. This project is going to stretch us to the limit, but I think we can get the house closed in and the barn up before snow flies. To help us reach that goal, we've decided to organize an old-fashioned barn raising.

Jude and I have noticed that while they won't discuss our so-called lost year, our families love the connectedness, vitality, and fun we have brought to their lives.

June 29, 1990 ∾

Barn-raising day—I'd say we did pretty well for a bunch of amateurs. The sun was going down while the last truss was going up. The rafters were all well braced by the time the darkness forced us to stop. The work was hard and the food was good (Mom's deviled eggs are even better than Hannah's pickled ones). We sang silly songs and told bad jokes. Our nieces and nephews played hide and seek all afternoon. Today, Jude and I could feel on Summer Hill the pulse of a day in the life of Kallimos. At one point late in the afternoon, we both stood back so that we could drink it all in. We wanted to say, "Don't you feel it all around you, don't you feel the *dohavkee,* the oneness?" We wanted to teach our families the songs we had learned, but we dared not. The moment passed, but at least we had the moment.

July 31, 1990 ～

Today, I made a major concession to this world. I went out and bought a chain saw. Actually, I think Jude's mom and dad see this as a hopeful sign that we're not totally crazy. I figure we'll need twenty to thirty face cords of wood to make it through the winter. I told Jude that I was sure I could do it all with an axe and a bow saw except for one problem—time.

Our house now has a definite outside and inside. We can boast of a complete set of doors and windows. The interior is nowhere near finished, but we can do most of that work during the winter.

Jude's garden is in full bloom. We knew the soil here was good. Unfortunately, it's also full of weed seeds. We spend at least two hours every day pulling weeds. The root cellar has been dug and the walls laid up from field-stone, but I still have to build the shelves we will need to hold our harvest.

Our construction projects have consumed our savings and all the royalties from The Book. Hence, I have taken a job as an emergency room doctor. I work three nights a week so that we can keep up with our bills. What I cannot do is work on the house, finish the barn, cut the firewood, and work in the ER. Hannah probably wouldn't approve, but it looks as if the chain saw is here to stay.

August 6, 1990 ~
Our first goats arrived today. They are yearling does, and I have named them Rose and Martha after the two I loved best on Kallimos. It feels good having them here.

September 26, 1990 ~
Our folks may doubt our stories about Kallimos, but they are impressed with Jude's way with a garden. The harvest is going to be huge, even though this is the first season the plot has been tilled. Just wait until next year.

Jude's pregnancy is really showing now. While we were working in the garden today, I tried to get her to rest on the porch. She would have none of it. She said, "Don't you remember the three sisters?" Still, I worry about all the heavy work she has been doing.

October 17, 1990 ~
We decided last week to celebrate King Aeon's Feast today. It's hard to make a feast with only two people, so

we both felt a bit let down. Jude and I talked about it, and we've decided that we'll teach our child all about the people of Kallimos and their ways.

December 9, 1990 ～
Today, a child was born on Summer Hill. Our daughter came into this world like a rolling clap of thunder. Her name is Haleigh. She is less than twelve hours old as I write this. I am a father now. I feel confused and over-whelmed by this new responsibility, but I know one thing for certain—our little girl is beautiful. Jude is tak-ing to mothering like a duck to water. She calms Haleigh with tiny kisses. My hope is that Haleigh will become as wise as the woman for whom she is named.

When a baby is born on Kallimos, the mother holds the baby close and composes a lullaby just for him or her. Later, the mother teaches the song to all of the peo-ple of the village. If everyone knows the song, then everyone can comfort the baby.

December 11, 1990 ～
Jude has taught me Haleigh's lullaby. It goes like this:

Hush, little baby girl,
No more tears.
Your Mommy loves you,
Know that she is near.

Hush, little baby girl,
You will grow wise.
Your Daddy loves you,
Now close your eyes.

Sleep now, little baby,
Your Mommy loves you.
Sleep, little Haleigh,
Your Daddy's near.

No more tears,
Little baby girl,
No more tears.

December 31, 1990 ∽

This New Year's Eve is bitterly cold. Jude, Haleigh, and I are spending the evening huddled beside our wood stove. Outside, the wind is driving the snow sideways. The snowdrift beside our door is already as tall as a person and growing.

Every couple of hours I venture out to the barn to check on the goats. They huddle together in the leeward corner of their pen, looking at me with the tepid curiosity of the truly contented. I've had to break the ice in the cistern each time I've gone out, and I usually freshen the hay in their manger. If we had electricity, I could plug in a bucket heater and save myself a lot of trouble. Still, given the weather, it's better to keep a close eye on them. There is no moon tonight, so I am making my way to and from the barn by the light of my kerosene lantern.

Our stove works well. There is an old saying that firewood heats you twice: Once when you cut it and once when you burn it. I can now testify to the truth in those words.

Jude is curled up on the couch next to me. She nursed Haleigh until the babe fell asleep, and now they both slumber peacefully. It is 9:30 in the evening. The only sounds I hear are the wind as it races beneath our eaves, the popping and crackling of the fire, and the soft regular breathing of my wife and child. We have made a good life here.

I should be perfectly happy, but I'm not.

My memories of Haleigh, Hannah, Zachary, and all our other friends are slipping away. Jude and I used to speak the language of Kallimos when we were alone. These days, we rarely do. I used to think that we switched to English because we were being lazy. Now, I'm not so sure. Speaking the language of Kallimos reminds us of what we have lost, of what we can never regain.

Jude and I have done our best to restore the wholeness and joy we found in Kallimos, but there is so much missing. It's true that I have my goats and Jude has her garden. What we do not have, however, is that wonderful sense of belonging, that sense of being embraced, that we had there. We are hungry for the shelter the people of Kallimos created for us. We are thirsty for the love, affection, and laughter they seemed to conjure from nothing. Here, we have set a banquet for the spirit, but we have no one with whom to share the feast. Without that, the food and drink seem less than nourishing, their taste less than satisfying.

Every now and then, especially when the weather is good, friends from our old life stop by to visit. They *ooh* and *ah* over the neatly stacked cords of firewood, the well-stocked root cellar, and the pungent goat cheese. We share a meal, and afterward they always ask, "When are you two going to get back to work?" They come prepared with job offers and not-so-gentle hints that we are wasting ourselves on this hill.

When they are gone, Jude and I struggle with the question of our future. "Should we leave Summer Hill? Should we go back to our old lives? Should we abandon the life and the lessons we learned on Kallimos?" A few days pass, and we don't call the numbers that have been left for us, and our lives continue. Still, I remember Hannah's last words to me: *When it is time for you to begin your work, I will come to you.* I have seen no sign of her, and so I continue to hide from a world to which I am no longer suited.

January 1, 1991 ~

The clock struck one and woke me. I must have fallen asleep, and now I must rouse Jude and get us all to bed. I hope that 1991 brings us less pain than 1990. How sad that the best I can hope for is a year of less hurt.

Tea with Hannah

January 26, 1991 〜

I'VE DECIDED TO BUY A TEAM of workhorses. A good, experienced team of geldings with harness and basic equipment is going to set us back about $3,000, and that means more nights at the ER to earn the money we need. The work is tolerable, and sometimes I even enjoy it. My biggest complaint is the hours. I hate working nights, but I'm unwilling to give up my days with Jude and Haleigh on Summer Hill.

I just finished four nights in a row, and tonight I get to reset my sleep cycle and go to bed at a decent hour.

January 27, 1991 〜

I had the most extraordinary experience last night— Hannah came to our house. It was so real that I'm willing to swear it wasn't a dream. I was sleeping when I heard someone saying, "*Firthen gritt bashtak costengunter*

198

tasha—Rise from your bed and join me, dear friend."

I opened my eyes, and there was Hannah, by the side of our bed. She asked me to join her for tea, so I followed her to the kitchen. She took the kettle, filled it with water, and set it on the stove. I sat at the table and watched as she opened the cupboard and took down the jar Jude uses for tea bags. The kettle whistled. I know I heard it whistle. She carefully made two cups of tea, and then she sat down and looked at me, just as she used to.

I told her about our return to this world, our visit to Montserrat's jail, and our reunion with our families. I told her about finding this land and building our home. I bragged about our daughter Haleigh and what a fine job Jude was doing of mothering her. All the while, Hannah listened, her deep blue eyes dancing as she heard my story.

When I stopped talking, she said that Haleigh missed having Jude at her side in the garden and that she would be thrilled to learn of her namesake. She told me Zachary had taken my place as the village goatherd. She described the antics that had occurred during the most recent King Aeon's Feast, and I laughed out loud. I asked about some of my favorite goats, but she didn't know the herd well enough to give me any specifics. It just felt so good to be with her. I reached out and touched her, and I could feel her warmth. She smiled at me for a moment when I did that and then looked into my eyes and said, "Do you remember when I promised to come to you here?"

"How could I forget?"

"I said that you and Jude had important work to do. The time has come to begin."

I looked away from her. She let the silence settle around us. I said, "I'm not ready, and neither is Jude."

"Your strength has returned," she answered. "You have been blessed, and now it is time for you to return that blessing."

"You may think that we're over the pain of losing you and the life we had on Kallimos, but we aren't," I told her irritably. "And we never will be."

"William, you of all people should understand that wounds don't disappear, they heal. Our wounds are part of who we are. We need them because they bear witness to the pain we have endured and the damage that has been done to us. They are precious to us because they help us tell our story to ourselves and to those we love."

"When we first met," she continued, "you said that you and Jude had great affection for the elders of this world. You said that you planned to spend your lives learning about them and sharing your wisdom with others."

I nodded silently.

"The lessons you learned on Kallimos can do much to improve the lives of the elders of this world. You have an obligation to share those lessons."

I stood up, put my cup in the sink, and turned back to her. "We can't do what you are asking us to do. We don't belong here anymore. This world moves in ways we can no longer accept. We have no place here." I struggled for words. "It's just . . . it's the way it is."

Hannah looked deep into her teacup as she considered my response. "If we had given you a powerful medicine that could cure cancer, would you share your knowledge of that remedy with the world?"

"You know I would."

"If you knew that someone else had been given that knowledge and had failed to share it with others, how would you feel?"

"About hiding a cure for cancer? That would be evil."

"So it would, but look at yourself. You have learned how to conquer the three plagues of loneliness, helplessness, and boredom. You and Jude have that wisdom bottled up inside you. It was entrusted to you as a gift from Kallimos to the elders of this world, and you are withholding it from them. Does the hermit's heart beat inside your chest? Are the elders of this world so unworthy that you can content yourself with your cozy little home?"

I fought for control of my emotions. How did this woman do it? She had cracked me open and guilt was pouring out. I shifted uncomfortably in my chair. The clock ticked behind us as I sat silent, torn between grief at what we had lost and guilt for what I had not done.

"I know," she said, softly, "how much you love stories, and I have one that may help you. You seem to think that your changed attitude about life in this world makes you an outcast, unable to teach others the lessons you have learned. I think the opposite is true. Haleigh taught me this story when I was a young woman just about to begin my work as a healer."

Long ago, when The People were new to this world, there was a small kingdom in the south of Kallimos. To the east lay the mighty, white peaks of the Pal-Chin Mountains; to the west, a broad, wine-dark sea. Good fortune had blessed the inhabitants of this land with a series of wise and gentle kings.

It was in the time of one such king that the inhabitants celebrated the birth of a prince. The king named him Sarop, and there was dancing in the streets as the news of his birth spread across the kingdom.

Now, for longer than anyone could remember, the inhabitants of this kingdom had made their way in the world by trading with the village of Tum-Bak-Tee, which lay to the east over the mountains. The path to Tum-Bak-Tee held great danger and required great courage from those who braved its narrow, twisting course. Stories of heroic mountain traders and their daring exploits were passed from generation to generation. Indeed, all the holidays of the kingdom revolved around the work of the traders. In the spring of each year, a great feast honored the opening of the pass, and in the autumn, another feast marked its closure.

This is the world into which Sarop was born. The young prince developed under the watchful eyes of his parents and members of the royal court. Almost from the day of his birth, they asked themselves, "What kind of king will he be? Will he be wise or foolish? Will he be peaceful or full of anger?"

The young prince gave his parents much to worry about. He showed little interest in the heroic exploits of the mountain traders, and he was slow to learn the songs that were sung of their deeds. When the time came for him to spend his time in the mountains to learn the duties he would perform as king, he slipped away and hid in the place he loved best—the dunes beside the sea.

Although the king and the queen, indeed the entire royal court, did their best to conceal his strange behavior, it was the talk of the kingdom. "Prince Sarop loves the sea," they whispered and shook their heads in disgust. Years passed, and in time, Sarop became king. He was a moody, unhappy ruler, and the inhabitants of his kingdom had little affection for him.

Then, one night, King Sarop had a dream. It woke him in the middle of the night. Indeed, the corridors of his castle were still dark when he snatched a torch from the wall and stormed toward his chamberlain's apartment. The chamberlain hauled himself out of bed to answer the king's frantic pounding. "Assemble my court at once," the king commanded and stalked off into the castle's gloom. The chamberlain did as he was told; by the time the first light of dawn was breaking over the eastern mountains, the court was assembled.

Sarop rose from his throne, cleared his throat, and said, "I will give 100 pieces of gold to any man who will swear to build for me an ocean-going vessel." He turned to his criers and to his messengers. "Take word of this to every corner and every crossroads in my kingdom. From Tiga in the north to Ogewo in the south, all must hear my words."

The conversation around that evening's fires had never been livelier. "A hundred pieces of gold! Can you imagine that? We'd be rich!" More reasoned voices cautioned, "It's a fool's dream, and it's bound to come to tears. People aren't meant to go to sea." So it was that on the day he was to award the gold, only three men presented themselves to the disappointed king.

Wearing a bearskin robe and a long, thick, dark brown beard, the patriarch of a great mountain trading clan stood tall and straight before the king. The portly royal carpenter stood to his left. He was fitted out in his best clothes for this rare visit to the court. To the carpenter's left, stood a cooper, a lowly barrel maker. Curls of shaved wood peaked out from the cuffs of his patched trousers. He clutched his cap in his hands and kept his head bowed.

The king handed each man a purple velvet bag containing 100 pieces of gold drawn from the royal treasury and told each that the vessels must be ready by midsummer's day.

That night, the patriarch of the mountain trading clan hosted a lavish feast. He plied his guests with wine, meat, ale, and cheese. He and his guests laughed at the foolish young king until their sides ached. "What a fool he is," they said, "wanting to travel on the sea!" The feast continued well past dawn.

The carpenter called all of his apprentices and journeymen to his side. "The king will make us rich," he said. "We'll build one vessel, and then everyone will want one." Although they had no idea how to build the vessel, the young carpenters delighted in the thought of the riches that would come from this royal folly.

The cooper sat at his supper table with his wife and children. He talked as he gulped down his stew and gnawed on the dense black bread that his wife had made. "Perhaps," he said to his wife, "the king is right to look to the sea. If I can make barrels that keep water in, surely I can make something that can keep water out." Before his family was asleep, he was hard at work in his shop.

When midsummer's day arrived, each of the boat builders presented his handiwork to the king. The patriarch smirked as Sarop examined his offering. That very morning, he had had his men lash a dozen or so rotten logs together with some moldy rope. The carpenter and his men bowed low and offered a delicate creation of the finest inlays and trim. The cooper stood nervously in front of his work, a giant barrel that was split lengthwise down the middle and laid on its side.

The king examined each offering in turn and then retreated to a nearby dune. As he stood there surveying the vessels, a blare of trumpets issued from the castle, and over the crest of the dunes stumbled the wives and children of the boat builders. Behind them were members of the king's guard. The crowd of courtiers fell silent as the families were marched at spear point to the waiting vessels.

"I asked each of these men," the king said, "to build an ocean-going vessel, and these are what they have made. Now it is time for each man and his family to put his work to the test." Each of the boats was loaded with the families and shoved roughly away from the shore. The ebbing tide carried them swiftly out of sight.

That night was the longest night in the history of the kingdom.

With the morning came the returning tide. The king was the first down to the shore. On the beach, cold and gray as the sea itself, lay the bodies of the patriarch, his wife, and their children. The king ordered that they be removed.

Next, he caught sight of the carpenter and his family. All that remained of the carpenter's work were the bits of flotsam they clung to. The king ordered that ropes be thrown to them, and the unfortunate souls were hauled to shore. They wrapped themselves in thick blankets and huddled around a hastily built fire.

Finally, the king's keen eye spied the cooper. He stood proud and tall at the tiller as his children gamboled about on the deck. As soon as the boat was secured, the king made his way to its side. The cooper knelt down as he saw the approaching king.

The king drew his sword from its scabbard, and the cooper quaked with terror. The jeweled blade glittered in the sun as the king raised it over the cooper's head and then brought it gently down on the man's trembling shoulder. "I make you, good Sir, a knight of my realm, and you and your children and your children's children shall build for me a thousand ships. With these vessels, our people will come to know every corner of this good earth. Now rise, sir, rise and begin your work." The king spoke in the loudest and clearest of voices.

Though the hands of time have removed even the faintest traces of the kingdom of Sarop from the face of Kallimos, The People still know his story, and when it is told, they always say, "That was the beginning of the age of Sarop the Great."

That is the way it was and that is the way it is.

"It is late, and you need your rest," I heard Hannah say when she finished her story. She guided me back to bed. I crawled between the covers, and she bent down over me. "*Dirn ramma rhee shost lorbay hubia cree*—May your rest bring to your heart the wisdom you will need for the morrow."

She was gone when I woke up.

The Birth of the
Eden Alternative

February 3, 1991 ~

I TOLD JUDE ABOUT HANNAH'S VISIT in the morning, and we have talked about little else since. It has brought us both suddenly and fully alive. We now agree that we must reach out to the world with what we have learned. Winter still has us locked in its grip, so we have plenty of time to prepare for what lies ahead. Jude thinks that the best way for us to get started is to pull together the ten lessons we learned. I think it would also help us to put the stories down on paper. We have spent the past few days in a frenzy of conversation and recollection. So far, we have resurrected six of the ten lessons and the stories of the three sisters, the treasure seekers, and King Aeon's feast.

There is so much more to do. It is clear now that I need to become involved with an organization that cares for elders. This will be the best way to learn how to place these lessons into practice. I am searching for an elder-care organization that needs a doctor.

After much conversation and debate, Jude and I have decided to call the lessons "The Eden Alternative." We are certain that this world needs an alternative to its conventional approaches to life and the elderly, and the story of Eden comes closest to the notion of life in a garden. When Jude reminded me that the very first example of a human problem is Adam's cry of loneliness in Genesis, that sealed it for me. Jude and I are going to teach the people of this world how to make gardens for their elders and themselves.

February 15, 1991 ~

We have two reasons to celebrate today. First, we have finally reconstructed all ten lessons and the stories that go with them. Second, I have been invited to serve as the medical director and attending physician for a very troubled nursing home near the hospital where I work. I am steeling myself for this challenge because I dislike nursing homes, and not just a little. I dread them. Still, this was the first position to become available, and I want to get started as soon as possible.

It is strange to realize that it was just two years ago today that our boat went down and we entered the world of Kallimos. A year ago, we rescued Zachary from the storm and were pulled back into this world. Tonight, we celebrated another new beginning. I am scheduled to begin my official duties at the nursing home on February 23.

Before we went to bed, Jude and I reviewed the ten lessons. Now we are certain that they are both correct and complete.

1. The three plagues of loneliness, helplessness, and boredom account for the bulk of suffering in a human community.

2. Life in a truly human community revolves around close and continuing contact with children, plants, and animals. These ancient relationships provide young and old alike with a pathway to a life worth living.

3. Loving companionship is the antidote to loneliness. In a human community, we must provide easy access to human and animal companionship.

4. To give care to another makes us stronger. To receive care gracefully is a pleasure and an art. A healthy human community promotes both of these virtues in its daily life, seeking always to balance one with the other.

5. Trust in each other allows us the pleasure of answering the needs of the moment. When we fill our lives with variety and spontaneity, we honor the world and our place in it.

6. Meaning is the food and water that nourishes the human spirit. It strengthens us. The counterfeits of meaning tempt us with hollow promises. In the end, they always leave us empty and alone.

7. Medical treatment should be the servant of genuine human caring, never its master.

8. In a human community, the wisdom of the elders grows in direct proportion to the honor and respect accorded to them.

9. Human growth must never be separated from human life.

10. Wise leadership is the lifeblood of any struggle against the three plagues. For it, there can be no substitute.

I am sure we can do this. All we have to do is teach the people at the nursing home these ideas, and the world there will begin to change.

Warming the Soil

ANOTHER LOUSY DAY. I don't know how much more of this I can take. Ever since the day I started work at that nursing home, I've figured that the place should be declared a federal disaster area and bulldozed into oblivion. The staff is cynical and openly antagonistic to the elders, to each other, and to the management. Every day, I am greeted by an outrage that exceeds all previous outrages. Every day, I shudder at the thought that I am guilty by association. I change my clothes when I get home from working there. Last Monday, I arrived to find broken beer bottles littering the floor of the elevator. Wednesday, we found mattresses and used condoms scattered about on the floor of an empty resident room. Yesterday, I went to see a dying patient and found the remains of last night's supper covering his sheets. Even worse, the stench told me that it had been quite some

213

time since those sheets had been changed. For God's sake, this is a human being. Today, I went on rounds, and we identified three new stage-four pressure ulcers. That brings the total to eleven. There is no reason for this.

The response to my protests? "We're short staffed, so that's the way it goes." Amazingly, the management is more dysfunctional than the staff. Whenever I want to talk to the administrator, I have to go outside and flag him down. He's been glued to the riding mower ever since the weather turned warm. Walking the halls is like entering one of the inner circles of hell. Living here must make many elders pray for death.

Our Eden Alternative means nothing to these people. We'll all go for a picnic on Mars before this place starts implementing the ten lessons.

How did I ever let myself become associated with this facility? How soon can I get out of here?

April 24, 1991 ∾

Three days ago, federal surveyors arrived for a surprise inspection. Today, they put the hammer down. They cited the facility for a half dozen extremely serious deficiencies. If the place doesn't do a major turnaround in ninety days, it will be closed. The staff will be let go, and the elders will be moved to different facilities. I say it's about time.

Jude was shocked when I told her. It was not the impending closure but my reaction to it that bothered her most. She seems to think that the Eden Alternative can still work some kind of magic with this place. She's upset that I have fallen into what she calls "a state of denial." That's easy for her to say—she doesn't have to work there. She wants me to hang tough, and I want to get out NOW. We had a long talk after supper and got no closer to a decision on what I should do. Fortunately, I have tomorrow off. I need time to think.

April 26, 1991 ~

The unseasonably warm weather of the past couple of weeks has been chased away by cold, damp air, overcast skies, and spring showers. After the milking yesterday morning, I told Jude that I was going for a walk. I grabbed my rain slicker, headed down the driveway, and turned onto my favorite dirt road with the rain falling hard on my back. I walked several miles before I decided to turn back.

As I turned around, I heard the sound of a car approaching from behind. I sidled over to the side so the car would have room to get past. I was surprised when it pulled up beside me and stopped. The front passenger's window rolled down and an old man peered out.

"Can I give you a ride, young fella?"

"No, thanks, I'm just out for a walk."

"You picked a hell of a day for it. Hop in."

"No, thanks, really. I'd rather just walk." I resumed my stroll.

Again, the car pulled up alongside me. "It's a mighty cold rain, and I've got the heat turned way up. Let me take you home."

I was starting to get annoyed. "I don't need your help. I'm fine, and if you'll just be on your way, I'll be able to get back to what I need to be doing."

I stalked off toward home, but I had gone no more than 25 yards when the car pulled alongside for the third time. The window went down, and I got ready to give the driver a piece of my mind. Instead, he gave me a piece of his—and it came in the language of the people of Kallimos.

"Damn it all, William, get in the car. Hannah sent me to find you, and if you don't get into the car, you're going to make me mad."

My knees began to buckle, and I clung to the car door with all my might. I answered the stranger in the same tongue. "Who are you? How did you get here? How do you know Hannah?"

"If you want to know more, I suppose you'll have to get into the car."

I pulled the door open and crawled inside, too stunned to say anything more. I looked closely at the driver. His face was lined deeply by decades of exposure to the sun and wind, and his jacket could not hide his enormous forearms.

"How do you know my name, and how do you know Hannah?" I asked.

"That would be a very, very long story, and one we don't have time for today. Hannah tells me that you're planning to run away."

I nodded dumbly.

"Seems that this whole business is harder than you thought it would be, isn't it? You thought you could just waltz right in, tack up the ten lessons, and everyone would leap to follow them."

His blunt truth made me blush. "Maybe that's so, but I still don't think I can put up with the garbage that's going on at that nursing home."

I slouched down into the seat while the old man mashed on the clutch, shoved the car into gear, and jerked the car into motion. As the sleeves of his jacket slid up his arms, I could see muddy blue blotches that must have been ancient tattoos.

"The trouble is that you don't really understand what you're doing," he said. "You've got the lessons written down on paper, and I suppose that's a good thing, but you'll be needing something more than paper if you want to change this world."

"Change the world? That's a joke," I scoffed. "I can't even make a dent in one pathetic little nursing home.

You know what the real problem is? All the ideas and all the stories of Kallimos make sense on Kallimos, but they don't make sense here. Here, the truth is all wrapped up in rules, regulations, dollar signs, and self-pity. Nobody has time for anything else."

The old man clucked his tongue softly as the car picked up speed. "Look, son, quit complaining, and remember that this is a broken world. If you stop blaming yourself for things that aren't your fault, you can get on with doing what's right and good. Hannah says your Eden Alternative is like a seed, but you should remember what happens when you plant a seed in cold soil."

"Cold soil? What does she mean, 'cold soil'?"

He smiled slightly as he peered through the rain on the windshield.

"Think, son. Think. The worlds we make for our elders and ourselves are like dirt. They can be warm and fertile, or they can be cold and frosty. Nothing grows in cold soil. You have to warm the soil." He rammed the car into second gear and popped the clutch. Both of our heads snapped back. "Damn this thing!" he complained.

If Hannah and this old man only knew how cold the soil was in this nursing home, I thought to myself. "All right," I conceded, "but how do I warm the soil?"

"Open hearts always come before open minds," he said with a shrug. He spoke as if this was the most common knowledge in the world.

"Okay," I told him. "I can see that I spent all my energy trying to pry these people's minds open. But what else could I do? I have no idea how to open someone's heart."

"Doing good deeds for a person and not expecting anything in return warms a heart," he replied. "Some people call it *mitzvah*; others call it *agape*. It doesn't really matter what you call it." We were fast approaching my driveway, and I didn't want the old man to miss it, so I pointed it out.

"I know where you live," he said with a wink. He swung the car into the driveway, pulled it down into first gear, and punched the gas. Soon we were pulling up alongside the house.

"Hannah says you've got a good heart, and Hannah is usually right. Things are going to work out. Just remember to warm the soil, and don't forget to listen to Jude. She's got the wisdom you're sometimes lacking. Listen to her, and your gardens will grow."

"I'll do that, I surely will, but I have to ask you— How do you know me? How did you get here? Can you take us back to Kallimos?"

He put his arm on my shoulder. "I can't take you back, at least not yet. The day may come again when the people of this world are able to see Kallimos and travel freely to her shores."

"When? When will that happen? How can we make that happen?"

"It will come to pass when the world relearns the wisdom of the ancients. You and Jude can bring that day closer. Teach the lessons of Kallimos, what you call the Eden Alternative, to this world, and every person who hears, understands, and acts on those lessons will bring Kallimos and this world closer together."

I felt like he had just asked me to bring him a tiger's whisker. I sighed.

"I'm sure Jude would like to meet you. Won't you come in for a minute?"

He twisted around while I was speaking, and he was fishing around on the floor behind my seat. "I'm afraid I can't do that."

I pushed the car door open and climbed out. "I understand, but just wait here a minute. I'll get Jude and bring her out."

He revved the engine as if to tell me that he needed to be on his way. Then he handed me a bundle wrapped in coarse paper. "Hannah told me to give you this. She said you'd be needing it."

I took it from him without looking at it. "Stay right here. I'll be right back." I raced inside, but by the time Jude and I made it back to the porch, the car and its mysterious driver were gone.

Inside, we unwrapped the package and found the journal I had kept on Kallimos. A note, written in Hannah's flowing hand, was tucked inside: "You must not let fear govern your hearts. There will always be a gap between what you wish to create and what you have created. That is as it should be. The way ahead is hard, but the day will come when many will share the work of the Eden Alternative with you. Work toward that day. When you are unsure what to do, seek guidance among the words you have written."

We reread the entire journal last night. Our tears splashed on many of its pages. When we finished, we knew, at last, that we were ready to begin the work we had been given.

Epilogue

January 1999

SOME OF THE EVENTS AND PEOPLE in this story are as real as the clothes on your back. Others sprang from my imagination. The difference between the two is unimportant. In truth, the distinction between the real and the imaginary frequently conceals as much as it reveals. Still, there are a few things I think you need to understand.

Jude and I have four children, with a fifth on the way. In this book, Zachary is named after our eldest child. Our Zachary bubbles with life and vitality just as he does in this book. He also loves to fish. Zachary is ten.

Virgil is named after our Virgil. He is wise, gentle, and full of patient understanding, just like the Virgil in the story. Virgil is eight.

Haleigh is named after our Haleigh. Haleigh came into this world carrying a heavy burden. Her doctors called it Idiopathic Infantile Encephalopathy. I still remember the day when they told us that our beautiful new daughter would never see, never walk, never talk. My heart broke that day, and it has never really been the same since. I was thinking of that when I wrote the following lines:

> "William, you of all people should understand that wounds don't disappear, they heal. Our wounds are part of who we are. We need them because they bear witness to the pain we have endured and the damage that has been done to us. They are precious to us because they help us tell our story to ourselves and to those we love."

We took Haleigh to the best pediatric neurologists in the world. They called her condition a one-in-a-million case of bad luck. Experimental treatments were worthless. We learned to love her as she was given to us, and she learned to delight our souls in the simplest of ways. Haleigh is five.

Hannah is named after our Hannah. The doctors who told us that Haleigh's condition was a rarity were wrong. Hannah has the same devastating neurological problems as Haleigh. In the story, we learn the most from Hannah; she is our greatest teacher. So it is in our family's life. Hannah has taught us the virtues of humility, forgiveness, and patience in masterly fashion. The pain of knowing that two of my children will never grow into lives of their own has gone deeper than any pain I have ever known. Yet, even in that pain, Hannah is there to teach me. In the story, I am often slow to understand Hannah. It takes me time to get past my own worried ego and grasp what she is trying to show me. I have lived this confusion; it is part of my life. Hannah knows that there is a life worth living to be found even in the midst of great affliction. Hannah knows the deepest corner of my heart. She is wise; she is two years old.

Jude is named after my Jude. Few are given the burdens she carries; yet, she carries them with honor and dignity. Few are given the blessings she had been given; yet, she shares them with grace and ease. She is strong when I am weak, and she is wise when I am foolish. While I have traveled far and wide to help others learn what we have learned, she has kept the roots of the Eden Alternative anchored in the warm, fertile soil that is our home. This book sprang from that soil, and she helped it to grow by giving me the time and freedom I needed to bring it to maturity. Thank you, Jude. You are the sun of my shadows, the light of my darkness.

Afterword

Jude and I started working with the ideas that would become the Eden Alternative in 1991. We found in nursing homes a human habitat so completely cut off from the living world and the virtues of love, trust, patience, and forgiveness that it cried out for change. Since then, we have helped hundreds of facilities make the difficult transition from institution to life-giving garden.

Now, increasingly, we see that the loneliness, helplessness, and boredom that cause so much suffering in nursing homes also afflict millions of people in the wider society. These are, indeed, the spiritual plagues of the modern age. Modern technology cannot cure or even blunt the suffering they cause. In fact, more often than not, the adrenaline-fueled rush of life in contemporary society aggravates their impact. The only solution lies in returning to ancient human wisdom. The secrets of a life worth living are all around us. They have been handed down to us across the generations, and they are intended for our use.

The principles laid out in this book are not new. In fact, they are very old. The challenge before us, then, is not one of discovery but of practice. How can we tame the modern system of industrialized work and materialist consumption before it subdues our spirits completely? How can we reassert our fundamental humanness in the face of modern life and all its challenges?

A poet once said the world is not made of atoms but of stories. Stories carry wisdom from person to person. They always have, and they always will. Our deliverance lies in the sharing of stories. For this reason, we have taken one step and ask you to take another.

We ask you to share this book with the people you work with, your neighbors, and your families. We ask you to discuss its stories and tell your own. Rediscover the richness and vitality that a night of spirited conversation and the sharing of stories can bring to your life. Imagine a world where the principles of Kallimos are woven into the fabric of everyday life. Then share your dreams with others.

Jude and I have created an online meeting place for those of you who want to continue the journey that way. It may seem odd to use the Internet to spread such ancient wisdom, but in this day and age we must use every means available to us to create and promote *dohavkee* connectedness in this world. Come to **www.kallimos.com** to tell your stories and read the stories that others are telling. Only by joining together can we find the strength we need to build a world where tenderness is valued more than violence, humility more that humiliation, and meaning more than money.

A Note
from the Publisher

If you are interested in learning how Dr. Thomas's vision translates to real situations in today's world, read his book *Life Worth Living: How Someone You Love Can Still Enjoy Life in a Nursing Home—The Eden Alternative in Action,* published by VanderWyk & Burnham and available through bookstores or by calling 1-800-789-7916.

Kallimos

The Great Desert

Mar-Kasha

Five Fingers
of Stone

Kahlid's Oas

Neekells

Shah-Pan

Kwa-Na-Na
River

Caleb's
Forest

The
Village

Village of
Rachael and Henry

Summer Hills

T

Zachary's Rock